Sophia James lives in Chelsea Bay, on the North Shore of Auckland, New Zealand, with her husband who is an artist. She has a degree in English and History from Auckland University and believes her love of writing was formed by reading Georgette Heyer in the holidays at her grandmother's house. Sophia enjoys getting feedback at facebook.com/sophiajamesauthor.

THEIR MARRIAGE OF INCONVENIENCE

Sophia James

MILLS & BOON

First Published in Great Britain 2020
by Mills & Boon, an imprint of HarperCollins*Publishers*
1 London Bridge Street, London, SE1 9GF

© 2020 Sophia James

ISBN: 978-0-263-27692-3

MIX
Paper from
responsible sources
FSC˙ C007454

This book is produced from independently certified FSC™ paper
to ensure responsible forest management.
For more information visit www.harpercollins.co.uk/green.

Printed and bound in Spain
by CPI, Barcelona

This book is dedicated to my father, Ron Kivell.
He, too, was an honourable man,
with a true moral compass, and I miss him every day.

Chapter One

~~~~~~~~~~~~~

London—July 1842

Miss Adelia Worthington knew how dangerous her plan was, but she couldn't turn back now, for when one was desperate, desperate measures had a need of being taken.

The door knocker was in her hand and she banged it thrice against a polished silvered strike plate. The servant who answered the summons looked about the street as if to understand the truth of a woman being so very alone here at this time of the night.

'I have come to see Mr Simeon Morgan.'

'Is he expecting you, miss?'

'He is not, but I know he is in residence and would appreciate a word.'

The clock in the hallway chimed out the

hour of ten thirty, underlining the question in the servant's face, and for a moment Adelia thought he might simply shut the door.

'I am Lady Worthington.' Perhaps if she used the status of her mother's title he might allow her access.

The name meant something, she could see that it did, for he faltered and stepped back, a blast of wind from the street helping to make up his mind.

'Very well, my lady. If you would follow me in, I will find you a seat and tell the master you require an audience.'

At that she almost smiled because he could not know that she required so very much more.

One moment later and perched on a chair of dark velvet studded in shiny brass buttons, Adelia looked around the room she was now in. The elaborate town house was exactly as she had expected it to be, full of pomp and richness, the furniture and curtains assaulting her senses. New money always screamed with a desperate need to be noticed and it was no different here, the colours of every expensive fabric, paper and wood surface clashing with the ones next to them.

If this was a tune, it would have been discordant and shrill. If this were a painting, there would have been no quiet subject peering out from within the frame. No, this excess was drawn in bold harsh strokes, the jarring and inharmonious risk of placing everything one owned on display for all to admire and marvel at. An unmeasured pretension that spoke of boasting and swagger and a certain self-importance.

She had expected it to be so, for Mr Simeon Morgan was one of the newcomers, his fortune made in clever investments in the freshly established railway lines destined to run the length and breadth of Britain. While many of his competitors were collapsing all around him with their over-optimistic speculations, he seemed to have forged ahead unscathed. By luck or acumen, she had no way of telling.

She longed for Athelridge Hall and its old-fashioned quiet colours even as her next thought overlaid that one. The Worthington estate could be gone from them completely and swiftly if this meeting did not go well.

A noise to one side had her looking up and a small girl stood there, her long dark hair plaited and one eye blackened.

Shock held Adelia immobile.

'You are very pretty.' The child's voice carried an accent from the north and the cut of her nightwear was not in the style of any servant's offspring. Mr Morgan's daughter, perhaps? My goodness, had he been married? Was he still? She had not heard a word about any union and horror consumed her at the very thought.

A flurry behind had another woman appearing, one who clearly had no compunction about grabbing the girl roughly and pulling her away. Should she say something? Should she demand from the older woman some assurance as to the child's welfare? Adelia stood to follow them just as the first servant returned with a calling card in his hands.

'Mr Morgan said that I was to give you this, Lady Worthington, after which I had to make sure you were safely escorted out to your carriage and seen off the property.'

All thoughts of the recent contretemps fled.

'He won't see me?'

'No.'

'If I sat here and waited…'

'He was most insistent, Lady Worthington.'

'Were I to return in the morning, would he be available then?'

'The master said that he would prefer any

contact with your family to be conducted through his lawyers. Their direction is stated upon the card you hold.'

She heard frustration in his answer at her continued presence here, and with more force than she meant, she tore up the card and let it flutter in small ragged pieces to the expensive Aubusson carpet below.

'Could you go back and tell your master that I have tried that avenue already and it has not been conducive to any meaningful dialogue. That is the very reason I am here. I should like to speak with him face to face so there can be no doubt as to what it is I wish to relate. It is a sensitive matter and not one for lawyers or third parties.'

'I am sorry, but I cannot allow you to go up, Lady Worthington.'

As the words echoed around the room, Adelia simply took a chance.

'Could you help me, please, for I am in great and desperate need? If you turned away for just one moment, our problem will be solved. That is all I ask. You do not need to do anything else but look away. I shall manage the rest.'

As he faltered, hope rose.

'I urgently need an audience. I promise I

shall tell Mr Morgan that I simply ran past you and up the stairs and that you had no way of stopping me, none whatsoever, even though you tried your very hardest. I will be off the premises in five minutes and after that I shall never bother anyone here again.'

'I could lose my job…'

'I would find you another.' She smiled in that particular way that seemed to send every man in society to pieces and saw him glance at her dimples.

'It is desperate, you say?'

'Completely and utterly.'

'Five minutes is all you require?'

'Not a second more. Please?'

The silence lengthened until he spoke again, this time in the slightest of whispers.

'Mr Morgan's chamber is the second door on the left at the top of the stairs, Lady Worthington. But he will not be pleased to see you, I can promise you that.'

Adelia simply took her chance and ran.

Simeon sat in the wing chair to one side of the low-burning fire and stared into the flames.

He was sick to death of the cold that had consumed him for over a week now, sending him every few moments into hacking bouts of coughing. He was sure a rib on his right-hand side was broken with the force of the paroxysms, and the fever which had been intermittent was back again, evident in the shaking of his chattering teeth. Even the thick woollen blanket pulled from his bed seemed to make no difference. He was utterly freezing.

'Damn,' he swore softly and laid a hand across his aching eyes.

He'd been asleep most of the day, which meant that he would be up all night. If he listened, he knew he'd shortly be able to hear the bells of St James's, Piccadilly, pealing out the third quarter. He wished it were dawn already even as he wondered why on earth Lionel Worthington's wife would come to visit him at this time of night. Lady Worthington? Was she mad? Did she expect clemency, or worse, forgiveness, for her husband's many sins? Harris, his butler, had said this visitor looked desperate and well she should. A man with the base morals her spouse had would distress any woman.

Leaning forward, he breathed out hard, trying to loosen the tightness in his chest. Well, his lawyers would soon see to her and send her on her way, that was what he paid them well to do. He tried to remember what Worthington's wife looked like, but could not recall her face at all. A blonde, he thought, and thin, but failed to find a true image.

Harris had conveyed his misgivings about this late and unexpected visitor succinctly.

'Lady Worthington looks a bit lost, sir. Like a stray cat.'

Well, the last thing he needed was yet another stray in his house, his thoughts going to Flora Rountree. The child had landed upon him out of the blue a week ago and he often heard her wails in his house at all hours of the night despite employing a well-turned-out and competent governess who came with glowing references.

'Damn it all.'

First the death of her mother, Catherine Rountree, and now this. The whole year so far had been a disaster and it was only early July.

The click of the door opening had him glancing up and, instead of his expected servant, the most beautiful young woman he had ever laid his eyes upon appeared. With teeth worrying her bottom lip, she let herself in and locked the door behind her, standing straight and determined after turning the key.

'Who the hell are you?'

His words made her frown, though the lines on her forehead took nothing away from her loveliness. Rather eyes the shade of emerald green only brightened and a mouth with full and sensual lips puckered with worry. He felt a tight clench of thrill in his stomach and shifted his position to dampen down the unwanted sentiment.

'Mr Morgan, I know I should not have come, but I have something to say to you that I cannot in all honesty enunciate to your lawyers or indeed to anyone else.'

Simeon drew up his blanket, wishing like hell he was better clothed.

'I am ill.'

He could not quite understand why he had said this, explaining away his lack of decent attire. After all, it was she who had crashed into his room uninvited and any account of his own actions was hardly an obligation.

She looked away, the candlelight catching her hair, strands of gold and wheat and pure-spun whiteness escaping from a hat of feathers angled across her head.

Had the fever made him delusional? Was she an angel descended from above and one who had landed fair and square in his bedchamber? Teasing him? Her next words dissipated that notion completely.

'My name is Miss Adelia Worthington. Lord Worthington is my father.'

'An unfavourable parentage then, though you look nothing at all like him.' He could not keep surprise from his words.

She ignored his comment and carried on. 'I have come to offer you a trade.' There was a quiver in the last word.

'A trade?' The room swam as he shook his head and listened.

'But first I need to know if you have a wife?'

'I have not.' The words slipped from him in disbelief. Where could this conversation be going?

'Good. The thing is that Athelridge Hall, the estate you gained from my father near Barnet, is my family home and all the property we have left in the world. I do not wish to lose it and so, as a way of mitigating the effects of my father's foolish investments, I have come to you with an offer of marriage.' She slowed down a bit now and swallowed. 'To myself, I mean. I am an innocent and I have had many proposals this Season for my hand. My success in the marketplace of high society has been well documented should you doubt what I am saying—an unequalled triumph, a victory of some worth according to all the sources that I hear it from.'

The words were running together now in a faster and faster way, no breath between the outpouring. He frowned.

'You are telling me that you are a prize, then? The incomparable Miss Worthington?'

'Indeed, many would say that I am.'

No false modesty deterred her from carrying on, although there was a new shake in her voice.

'In exchange for what I offer you, I want you to gift me Athelridge Hall. As my husband it would still be yours to all effects and purposes and I understand that. But my home would be safe and I would still have the rights to it. So it is something barely noticeable for you, not even an inconvenience. I know how rich you are and that the estate represents an insignificant investment for you, but I should not expect a share in anything more than Athelridge Hall. Ever.'

'My God, you cannot be serious, Miss Worthington?'

He saw her fingers close around a small gold cross that she wore on a chain around her neck as if to counteract his blasphemy as she continued.

'But I am, Mr Morgan. I should allow you your full rights as a husband as well as your prerogative to choose a mistress. Any number of them. I should not stop you from…making your own personal choices. I would be compliant, dutiful and discreet. I would run the estate with diplomacy, refinement, grace and tact. Even if you stayed only one night a year at Athelridge Hall I should not complain and I would not expect you to bring me to London. Whatever you wanted I would attempt to give to you. Without complaint. In short, I would endeavour to be the perfect wife. Tolerant and accommodating. Barely there.'

'A comprehensive promise?' He could not believe the absolute inappropriateness of her making such a pledge to him.

'And one you might favour?'

He laughed. 'You know nothing about me, Miss Worthington. How old are you?'

'Nineteen.'

'A baby. Go home and thank the Lord for your lucky escape.'

When her eyes darkened and flashed fire it heartened him. Not quite a docile martyr, then? She certainly wasn't doing as he had bid her either. The deep dimples in both cheeks as she bit at her lip unsettled him, for they were apparent even when she did not smile.

'Every other unmarried man in society and many of the married ones hold a great desire for me. Why would you not?'

'Because I have no wish whatsoever for a wife, even one as compliant and long-suffering as the model of the one you are promising me. I fare far better with more disposable lovers, mistresses and courtesans. I can change them whenever I am bored, which I often am. Without drama. Without question. Here today, gone tomorrow, so to speak. An impermanent liaison which requires no true commitment and has the added benefit of hurting nobody.'

He stood and crossed the room to pour himself a brandy, the warmth of it suppressing the shivers he could feel returning. 'Given the indisputable fact of your glowing first Season, every other man of your acquaintance is probably better suited to your needs than I am. Go away, Miss Worthington, and pick one.'

'No.'

That word was whispered, but he had already heard enough. She was like a small exotic bird who had strayed into a lion's den. How did she not realise the danger she was in?

'That is more than enough. Scurry back to your besotted society suitors, the ones who would fit into the lifestyle you are more than used to, the ones who would welcome such a broad and extraordinary promise and honour it as I would not.'

He could see the worry on her face, but he could also easily understand her effect on any man who came across her. She was the most exquisite female he had ever known. Unforgettable. Fragile. And beautiful beyond words. He could barely keep his gaze off her face and he hated himself for such shallowness.

'That is impossible, Mr Morgan, for the home I had, Athelridge Hall, is now your own and I need it back.'

'Did your father direct you to come here?' God, Simeon could almost imagine it of the man. To sacrifice a daughter for the mistakes he had made and would keep on making. To muddy the pond with compromise and immorality and think nothing at all of it. To send another in his stead to accomplish his dirty work.

The blood fled from her face at his query and he thought for a second that she might simply fall to the floor, but her hand found the brass bedstead and then she didn't.

'I came of my own accord, sir.'

'A risky business that, given the enormity of your proposition, the smallness of your person and the lateness of the hour.'

'Sometimes safe and easy pathways are unable to be…found, and one has to forge a new way.'

'With all your many stated and ardent proposals my advice to you would be to use such lofty options and make a choice. Find a lord of means who might appeal to you and marry him summarily as protection.'

Another flare of anger brightened her eyes. She had secrets, Simeon thought. He recognised them easily in others.

'You are the only person who holds the titles of my family home in your pocket, sir.'

'Then tell your papa to come up with the money and I will consider selling them back to him. Even a plan for repayment will do me fine.'

The beginning of tears surprised him.

'That is impossible.'

She was so young, Simeon realised suddenly, and simply had had enough. Better to frighten her, then, and send her packing in shock. His past was hardly salubrious and the mystery surrounding him would help see her on her way.

'I am not paying the high price you ask for the virginity you mention, Miss Worthington. However, if indeed you do feel the need to show me the goods I wouldn't object in the slightest...'

He let the sentence slide, knowing the insult within them, but he needed her gone.

'The goods?' Her cheeks flamed red.

'Tempt me with your breasts, your hips, your crinkum-crankum. All the parts of a woman that attract a man and make him sell his soul. Unbutton your bodice and surprise me.'

The grubby slang had her eyes widening just as he knew it would. 'I do not think...'

'Don't think, Miss Worthington, just go.'

The fury in him was building because he understood what was at stake here and how carefully her father had orchestrated such a travesty. Lionel Frankton Worthington was a bastard and if his daughter had failed to realise it then she must be of the exact same mould. It behoved him to punish them both by exposing such a crude proposal, though he knew of course that she would run now, from his presence, from his house, from his life, and she would never come back. He waited for her footsteps, exhaustion vying with rage.

When shaking fingers came up to the buttons at her bodice, his heartbeat skipped. He saw then an undergarment of silk and lace across milk-white skin, rising flesh and pink-tinged nipples. When she moved again the curve of womanhood and a round abundance of softness was clearly visible above her fallen clothing.

Behind her the clock struck the hour of eleven. The hush grew and grew as his eyes feasted on her bounty, there for such an easy taking, there to reach out and seize. He could have Miss Adelia Worthington in a moment. She was her father's daughter, after all, and payment was much more than overdue.

He scowled as his body hardened, cursing the betrayal even as he welcomed it. This was not going anything like he thought it would, yet he could not turn away. When he stood he let the blanket around him drop as he took the first step towards her. Damn the consequences, he thought savagely, he had never been a saint, after all, and if the beautiful daughter of his worst enemy had done her homework she would have at least known that.

He was a huge man and dark, the tight trousers he wore moulded around his body like silk, the white shirt above unbuttoned all the way down the front. In the shadows of the fire and the night he looked like Hades escaped from his Underworld, a dark soul-taker bent on her destruction. She should have run when he had allowed her the chance, but if this failed…

He stopped a foot away and reached out, one finger trailing across the underside of her right breast before settling on the nipple. The heat of him was as shocking as that in the room and she knew if he wanted to he could ravish her here and now and she would never be able to halt it. He was crude and coarse and his accent was a strange one, clipped in a careful way as though hiding all that he had been, once.

Yet she was caught in the glance of his golden eyes and rendered speechless by his sheer masculine presence. The digit moved, up and down, evoking a visceral response and, for the first time in her whole life, Adelia understood the meaning of lust. Her breath shallowed and her head tipped back, the place between her legs sliding into something between a throb and an ache. Formless. Unshapen. Lost.

Amorphous. Like a tide, the high swell of it tipping her over.

She held no touchstone, no way of stating the wrongness of all that was happening to her because in this moment it only felt right. She was held captive by forbidden delight and by a man whom she had never known the likes of.

Then his hand trailed up across her throat and on to her cheek before it traced the line of her upper lip with a precise and careful tenderness.

He made no move to come forward, though, even as she hoped he would, this stranger with his unshaven face, his darkness and his heat.

He had turned down marriage and offered her this, yet even with her breasts unbound and on show he did not simply take. She needed to say something, needed to make it matter, the ache of the sensual and the certainty of his want.

Swallowing, she tried to shape her words.

'Marry me, Mr Morgan, and…you can have it all…this…everything… I promise and without argument.'

The nipple his hand had returned to was swollen as he dipped to take the hardness of it into his mouth, hot suction drawing out a moan before he broke the pressure. Utter desire snaked through every part of her—fire, hot and undeniable.

'I could have you anyway and easily, Miss Worthington, for your body is telling me so.'

'No.' But she could not find any resistance within her as his tongue flicked back against her, a different movement now, a stab of pure passion assaulting her senses, her flesh moving in the rhythm he inspired, the wet warmth inside bursting through in waves and building, higher, deeper, longer.

The stubble on his cheek scratched her skin and the hand that held her anchored was tight on her flesh.

She was someone else, someone brighter and bolder, someone who would take the risk and use it, feel it, know it. The mystery and the danger and pure unadulterated need drove fear away and welcomed in a languid floating relief which brought tears to her eyes.

He caught her as she lost balance and held her close, his breath in her hair, rough and fast, as if he, too, had been surprised by this.

This?

What had happened?

Already the horror was building and the disbelief.

Her father had been a man who used women for pleasure again and again with no thought for a wife at home or a family who understood that their papa was not quite as others were. Was she of the same mould, a daughter who had come here with a ridiculous plan and expected this man to fall at her feet and agree to it?

An immoral woman. One who might trick others with her body and imagine no redress. A stupid, vain and foolish woman who had anticipated her beauty would be enough?

Already he had let her go and for that at least she was glad.

Adelia Worthington stood there, her mouth open and her emerald eyes glassy, the palpable beauty that had been so obvious before glittering now under another truth.

Wanton. Shameless. As good as any of the whores he had bedded with her quicksilver metamorphosis, nipples hard, lips swollen, breath shaky.

'Dress yourself, Miss Worthington.'

He could not be kind. He felt used and tricked and sullied somehow. An evening meeting that had taken only moments to draw down into this. She had done it before, no doubt, the virgin ploy sending him off guard and her unmatched comeliness seeing to the rest.

He could smell her scent from here, all woman and eagerness.

'God.'

The fever seemed to have risen and the heat in the room made him sweat. Her breasts stood firmly round and pale in the light, her fallen bodice still exposing everything. Beautiful beyond measure.

He saw the marks of redness on her skin, marks where he had sucked too hard in unparalleled ardour. The slender column of her throat lay unprotected, blue lines just beneath the skin. Fragile. Dangerous. Spellbinding. Menacing.

Was she here at the behest of her father to blackmail him in some way?

He half expected the Viscount to hammer down the door and demand retribution. If he had not been so sick he would have seen the trap of it in the very first seconds, but fever had softened his sense.

'I am not the husband you are after. There is nothing I can offer you save, perhaps, pity.'

'Pity?'

'Your father? You must realise the loathing he inspires among all who have the misfortune to cross his path? Tell him I know exactly how Catherine Rountree died. Tell him that his mistress left me a letter explaining things. Tell him that all of London shall soon know what he has done and he shall be pilloried for it. Tell him he cannot sacrifice his daughter to escape retribution, even such a daughter as you.'

She swallowed and pulled up her clothing, the shaking worse now than it had been before, the gold cross at her neck glinting.

He had had enough of lies. His own lies. Catherine's lies. Lionel Worthington's lies. Death held some reckoning and the child fostered upon him demanded recompense. From them all.

'I am sorry—' she managed to say before he interrupted her.

'Don't be.' He turned away as the words came out brokenly. He didn't want excuses or vindication. He wanted her gone.

When he looked back again there was no one there, the only sign of her ever being in his room a lingering perfume of lemon and lavender.

He'd expected more complex scents. The simplicity of what was left felt jarring somehow and he wished like hell that she had never come. Laying his arms on the marble of the mantel, he dropped his head against the cold stone, hating the shaking that was back and the fear within him.

Chance was something that seldom happened without a strong reason and her intent had held little of the coincidental within it. No, Miss Adelia Worthington had come here with a fully formed purpose and one that he feared she would not simply abandon. He would hear more from her, he knew it, but next time he would be ready.

Another darker thought also struck him, now that the fog of desire had lifted. There had been bruises on her arms and on the back of her neck. Substantial bruises that gave the impression of great force. Who had hurt her and why? Secrets wound into conjecture and puzzlement came in on top of that. She was a mystery, this beautiful and young Miss Adelia Worthington, and one he did want to unravel, damn it.

Once outside Adelia thanked the Morgan servant for accompanying her to the waiting hackney, smiling at him in a false and desperate way that set her own teeth on edge.

'Thank you for the chance to see Mr Morgan. I am sorry I was longer than five minutes.'

'It was a pleasure, my lady. I hope you accomplished all you wished to.'

She did not answer, for she knew without doubt that she was now ruined.

Mr Simeon Morgan would tell everyone about her foolish and dreadful mistake and society would turn their backs upon her and give her the cut direct. She could not even begin to contemplate the consequences of such a public exposure.

It was over. Athelridge Hall was lost. Her family would be homeless.

She should have taken the other pathways

open to her. She should have accepted the proposal of the first even slightly wealthy suitor who had offered for her. She had not hated any of them in the way she hated Simeon Morgan, the rich and amoral spawn of the devil. He had baited her, she knew that now, and she had risen to his words like the imprudent girl she'd thought she wasn't. He was never going to consider her ridiculous offer, not even for a moment. Her arm ached and the marks on her breast stung in shame.

Yet below this another thought harboured and her nipples rose into nubs at the echo of it. She had wanted him to touch her. She had wanted what she had seen so briefly in his golden eyes as his mouth had come down roughly across her breast. Wanted the passion in him, the desire and the hunger.

He was a rake and a womaniser, exactly like her father, though at least he was honest in his admitting of it. He'd told her she was a baby and that he bedded only mistresses and courtesans. He'd said she should run before she got hurt and that he could offer her nothing save pity.

Yet pity was not the emotion she had seen on his face just before she had left. No, there was anger there and fury mixed with aggravation and stronger things. Fiercer sensations.

The world crashed down over complications even as the body of her father was becoming cold on the floor of slate in the front room of Athelridge Hall.

His servants would find him tomorrow, the old Cranstons, in the first morning light and he would be lain in state, three handfuls of salt sitting on his chest on an earthenware plate and a portrait of the Virgin Mary hung above giving spiritual guidance. These would be her mother's instructions, her Scottish heritage fully formed in the art of death.

If it had been left to Adelia, she would have had no compunction in tossing him out to be buried in a beggar's grave in some unknown churchyard. And she would never have visited it afterwards.

Chapter Two

Viscount Worthington was dead.

Simeon had heard the news today, six days after his daughter's outrageous and unasked for late evening visit.

Dead from suicide.

Simeon wondered about his part in the whole conundrum given his lack of care in allowing the man's offspring title to the small and insignificant Athelridge Hall estate. But still he could not be sorry. If the Viscount had killed himself over his foolish loss at his ill-played games of investment, then the world was better off for it. If he had killed himself in remorse for the accident with Mrs Catherine Rountree on the Northern Road, then at least he had died for something more honourable.

Privately, Simeon felt the motive of greed

was more likely to be the reason for his death than that of principle, but he didn't care enough to give the dead man any benefit of the doubt.

Beneath him, Theodora Wainwright was pliant and generous. Her long red hair streamed across the white of the pillow in fiery threads and her eyes, while not the startling green of Miss Adelia Worthington's, were none the less alluring enough.

He liked the feel of her, he liked her smell. But most of all, he liked the way she demanded nothing of him.

Small and even white teeth nipped at his shoulder.

'Your mind is far, far away, Simeon. Am I not enough of a distraction for you today? Would you like other…ministrations?'

She licked his ear as she said this, her fingers closing around his manhood. 'I have two hours before I am needed anywhere else and I still harbour a lot of inclination for more of your body.'

Such thoughts began to work upon his libido and he felt a rising. Damn Worthington and his ill-timed demise, damn his comely daughter for her unsettling visit and damn his own mind for spending so much time ruminating upon them both.

Turning Teddy over, he brought his mouth down across one large breast. At thirty-five Theodora was a woman who knew her own body and she was rabid in her demand for satisfaction. An experienced female, proficient in the art of lovemaking, the two husbands she had lost young added to her allure. She would never marry again. She had told him this daily when he had first met her a year ago, though lately she had said it less and less. A small throb of warning halted him, but she was not having that, her fingers now in other places, clever and slick.

'Take me, Simeon, and ride me high and long. Make me scream in bliss.'

The dirty talk was working and she was already wet with their endeavours from half an hour earlier. Without a word, he entered her and thrust on home, her face dissolving into relief and her nails clawing into his skin, drawing blood.

Pain and passion. An avid mix. He lifted her up and rode her as she had requested, her shouts of delight muted by his fingers hard banded across her lips.

* * *

Three hours later he was sitting at the back of a pub in Regent Street, the place filled to the brim with rowdy locals, the smell of smoke and strong drink in the air.

Tom Brady, one of his oldest friends, was waiting for him, two cold beers on the table. He was an inspector for the Metropolitan Police and a damn useful contact to have.

'I got your note, Sim, and I looked into the fiasco of Worthington's last few weeks on this earth.'

'And?'

'The Viscount actually died a few days before the family released the news, apparently. On the eighth of July.'

Simeon counted back the days. If this was true, then the Viscount was dead already when his daughter had come to see him and yet she had hardly looked grief stricken. Why not?

Tom Brady continued. 'Lionel Worthington was rumoured to be all but bankrupt and his sole estate is not even in the family's hands after he made a number of poor investments. There is also talk of his late mistress, Mrs Catherine Rountree, for some say the Viscount had a hand in her death a month ago. He drank a lot by all accounts and a few of the first people on the scene of the carriage accident in the north intimated that he looked demented. An angry drunk, they told the constables who finally arrived, though by that time Worthington was long gone. Skulked off into the shadows in his drunken fury, hiding until he could formulate more lies to make some sense of his disappearance and be exonerated.'

Fury railed in waves across Simeon's body.

'A letter, written by you, was found among the Rountree woman's effects at her house in Camberwell, by the way, Simeon.' Brady dug around in his pocket. 'I thought you might like it back before anyone else could use it to point the finger at you, so to speak.'

Taking it, Simeon held the missive tight while he struggled to work out what to say.

In the end he stuck with the truth.

'Did you read it?'

'I did.'

'Did anyone else?'

'No. The property of the deceased Mrs Catherine Rountree was still to be sorted. A letter like this, where you threaten the Viscount, might be inflammatory for there were things about the Viscount's death that did not make sense.'

'Things?'

'One of the Worthington servants, when questioned, said he heard raised voices and a fierce argument well into the evening. He thought perhaps there had been a visitor in the house, for around midnight he found the front door ajar, banging in the wind, and he was certain that it had been secured earlier on, as it always was.'

'Who do you think it was?'

Tom shrugged. 'Worthington had his enemies. It could have been any number of people, but our services are stretched and there are other more important cases that will take precedence. You didn't see him into the next world, did you, Sim? Your missive held threats, after all.'

Lifting the beer to his lips Simeon drank deeply before replying. 'Viscount Worthington wouldn't be worth spending a long time in gaol for.'

'From memory, you knew his mistress, Mrs Catherine Rountree, well, though, did you not? I recall you mentioning her over the years.'

'She grew up in Angel Meadow, too, which

is why I have taken full responsibility for her little child.'

'Some say that Lionel Worthington was not kind to the girl, thinking her only a nuisance who took up far too much of Mrs Rountree's time.' When Brady spoke again there was hesitation in his words. 'Did you see the Viscount in the days before his untimely demise, Sim?'

'I did. I felt so strongly on the subject that I followed up my letter with an ultimatum in person the morning before he died. I reiterated that if he ever went near Flora Rountree again I would kill him. I was pleased to hear he went home and saved me the bother of seeing through such a threat.'

'His older daughter found him.'

'I had not heard that.'

'It isn't common knowledge. He is buried at Athelridge Hall apparently, in the small graveyard to one side of the chapel.'

'Who is the heir to the title?'

'A Mr Cartwright from York. Word has it he has a much bigger estate up north and Athelridge Hall was never part of the entailed property.'

'So the Worthington family have returned home?' Simeon thought of the deeds of ownership to Athelridge Hall sitting in his wall safe and the reality of an eternal resting place for a man he'd hated being right under his nose.

'They left London in a rented hackney and the bills from their lengthy stay here have been left unpaid. Everyone is speaking of it so I doubt Miss Adelia Worthington will have any more suitors arriving on her door-step now.'

'You know of her?'

'Miss Worthington?' Tom hesitated, looking at him in a strange way. 'What man with eyes and ears in London would not? Her beauty is heralded as unsurpassed and if her character has defects, then who would notice them?'

'Defects?'

'Apparently, she is haughty and strong minded and has turned down each and every desperate suitor with barely a reason. As a con-sequence, we at the Metropolitan Police have been foiling planned duels in her name ever since the end of January, when she arrived in the city.'

'Like a modern-day Helen of Troy; a face that has launched a thousand proposals?'

Tom laughed, but all Simeon could think of was one proposal. Hers to him. *'I will allow you anything.'* The very words made his loins ache, a further irritation in a difficult month. His fever had abated, but the heat of their re-membered encounter had left him unfathom-ably and uncomfortably warm.

'Could I ask you to settle the debt the Worthingtons have left behind them in Lon-don, Tom? Anonymously.' He brought out a wad of notes and peeled them off. 'This should cover it. Speculation and gossip about that family will only harm the small daughter of Mrs Rountree if anyone were to dig deeper. Any investigation into Worthington's liaisons means the child may be questioned and I'd rather she wasn't.'

Taking the money, Tom shoved it into his waistcoat pocket. 'I'll do that, though there is something else, too, that I need to speak to you about. Something much more…personal.'

His tone had Simeon looking up.

'Is Lionel Worthington's older daughter a particular friend of yours?'

'No. I only met her once a week or so back under difficult circumstances, but I barely know her.'

'Then you might be interested in the fact that Miss Adelia Worthington has told everyone you asked for her hand in marriage and that her father had given his blessing. His last rite as a parent, I think she said, and the first time in a long while that she had seen him happy. A final gift. Something to be treasured.'

'Are you serious?'

'She has the proof, too, for her matrimonial dowry was Athelridge Hall and she has made it known that you accepted the titles for it from the Viscount as surety of your intentions.'

'I recovered the place after Worthington's bad investments began to impinge on my own portfolio.'

Tom frowned. 'Was it a public notice?'

Simeon did not answer.

'Witnesses would have been useful, but still…' Tom threw that thought away and began on another. 'Her beauty must count somewhat in her favour.'

'Favour?'

The way Tom had said that sentence was somewhat worrying.

'She is a tease, so I'm told, and a woman who provokes gossip. If Miss Worthington's first months in society were filled with offers from the smitten sons of society, her last one was not. She hit the Honourable Rodney

Anstruther over the head with an umbrella in Hyde Park for no good reason whatsoever and he has made certain everyone knows of it.'

'What does he say of her, then?'

'That Miss Worthington has an icy heart and a cold manner and that she is not to be trusted.'

The day drew in on him.

'And the others?'

'Have withdrawn their own suits on the death of her father. It seems that the Worthington financial stability is not at all as the Viscount had intimated and society favours the wealthy. Perhaps Adelia Worthington has her own reasons for her interest in your substantial fortune, Sim. A solution, so to speak, to all her woes.'

Just like all of the others. Just like the newly brought-out debutantes and their desperate mothers. He'd been in society just twice over the past year and had hated it both times. It was why he had stuck with Theodora Wainwright and her ilk. While such women might wish for permanence in his life, they would never expect it.

There was no way in hell that Lionel Worthington and his daughter would have the last laugh. No. He would visit his lawyers tomorrow and find out just what could be done to escape these lies.

With a flourish, he finished his beer and called for another just as Tom began to speak again.

'You're twenty-seven now, Sim. Some wily female would have caught you sooner or later and you need heirs for that fortune you have accumulated.'

Simeon shook his head. 'You are wrong about that. A fortune means nothing to me and one marriage in this lifetime was more than enough.'

Tom nodded. 'Hell, I had almost forgotten about Susan Downing. What were you? Nineteen?'

'Led by my lust and eminently stupid is what I was. I regretted marrying her the morning after we had walked up the aisle. With Miss Worthington there wouldn't even be that twenty-four hours of hopefulness.'

'You could leave England. Disappear for a while?'

'I have a business to run. I'd be as bankrupt as Lionel Worthington if I did that.'

'Then if there is no way to escape marriage, take her to Athelridge Hall and leave her there. There are many other men in London who never see their wives and life goes on as normal.'

'Normal?' Simeon could hardly get his head around the very idea. 'A misguided deceitful harlot claiming my name and bearing any rightful heir. How could that ever be normal?'

The cold he was recovering from suddenly seemed to freshen and he spent the next few moments coughing, sick in mind and body and reeling from the betrayal of a girl who wasn't even out of her teens. If he handled this crisis badly, he would be the laughingstock of London and his burgeoning investment business would bear the brunt of his ill-thought-out decisions.

Already his youth in the founding of a railway empire had counted against him and he did not need this sort of a mess in his personal life to add to any conjecture. This industry depended on steadfastness. It needed a cool head and a sound grasp of financial practice. A humiliating and contentious marriage would be the antithesis to all he had worked so hard for and there was no way he would let such a thing happen.

No. Miss Worthington might not yet realise that she had a tiger by the tail with his claws unsheathed, but she soon would.

A private battle it might have to become, but he could well deal with that. He swore that she would rue the day she had tricked him into this and the most beautiful visage in all the world would be no protection whatsoever against his unbridled fury.

Fifteen hours later Simeon swept through the gates of Athelridge Hall, outside Barnet, in his carriage with all the speed of a man with the devil on his heels. And in a sense an evil spirit was there in front of him, in the form of Miss Adelia Worthington, a tease, a liar and a hypocrite. He'd had his lawyers look over his alternatives and paying her off seemed like the easiest and least public option.

Even the thought of parting with some of his hard-earned fortune made him absolutely furious, especially in the face of such baldly executed lies, but marrying her and living a lifetime of deceptions and fabrications again looked a whole lot worse.

He had dressed in his most sombre suit of clothing, a dark wool that he'd paid too much for from Henry Poole in Brunswick Square. He was glad of the no-nonsense cut of the jacket even as he loosened his necktie a little. He would need all the certitude that he could muster, all the righteousness his career had honed and perfected. His best game without a doubt was called for and the utter disbelief and rage in the face of Miss Worthington's deceit must be somehow bridled by sense and substance. And also by the cold hard cash of blackmail if it came down to that.

He could ill afford to show her exactly how incensed her falsehoods had left him feeling because it seemed that Miss Worthington held no compassion or empathy for anyone or anything.

His lawyers, too, had been most specific. Without witnesses to his acquisition of the family estate the daughter had a clear case of intent of purpose and, in all likelihood, the law would most probably side with a wronged and young female of good birth. Her beauty held some account, as well. It seemed she'd had suitors falling at her feet after only a few seconds in her company and any legal opposition would most probably succumb to such feminine persuasion. She would be absolutely lethal in court.

A doomed rebuttal. A closed case. Unless he was generous and clever.

The servant who came to the door was ancient, a wizened octogenarian of indeterminate hearing and sight.

'I need to see Miss Adelia Worthington immediately.'

'Pardon, sir. Speak up a little so that I might hear you better.'

At this the man took a step to his left and lifted up a piece of paper rolled into the shape of a cone and proceeded to apply the small end to his left ear.

'Talk into this if you will, sir.'

'Miss Adelia Worthington.' Simeon shortened his sentence and waited.

'You wish to see her?'

Instead of answering, he simply nodded and watched as the man shuffled off.

The place was tatty and worn, the wallpaper to the left of the door peeling away into long unfurling strands. No one had seen to it in years, he surmised, as he spotted small parts of the detritus all over the cracked tiled floor. In fact, nothing looked cared for or well-tended.

Wrath warred with disbelief, the two emotions producing a third feeling of sheer puzzlement until he felt as if he might well burst with the mix.

Fisting his fingers, he tried to pull himself together. He'd survived a childhood of sharp edges and was now a bulwark of sound English business practice. He'd become a man who was frequently held up as a shining example of wisdom and astuteness, yet within a moment of coming anywhere near to the person of Miss Adelia Worthington he seemed to have lost all good judgement and prudence.

She arrived as he took in a sharp breath, an old cloak wrapped around her body and a look on her face that held only horror. Simeon did not give her the chance to speak first.

'I will not marry you, Miss Worthington, and if you have the temerity to think your mean-spirited trick might actually work and imagine that I should bow down to such treachery, then you do not know me at all.'

The old servant stood beside her, watching his lips as he spoke, a heavy frown forming on his lined face. Another elderly woman of the same ilk had come to observe them from the head of a dark passageway and she looked just as concerned.

Adelia Worthington remained speechless, the

startling beauty of her face like a red rag to a particularly temperamental bull. Her hair was largely down and undone and she had smudges on both cheeks. Even dirty and unkempt she was an Incomparable and he thought she must know it for she had the gall to actually smile at him.

'If you would step into the sitting room, we could continue our discussion there, Mr Morgan...'

'Discussion?' He heard the anger in the word as he responded.

'Argument, then,' she gave back with a quiet reserve, 'and an argument I would prefer was for our ears only.' She stated this as he simply stared.

Good Lord, he had seriously underestimated her. She was as proficient as a high court judge in trying to defuse a difficult situation. She was even now ordering a pot of tea to be brought in.

'I think absinthe might be more my drink of choice, Miss Worthington. An elixir associated with social malaise and personal violence seems to be in order.'

She ignored that and added sweet biscuits to her list of wants, the old woman waiting by the door scurrying off to fetch them, the even older man at her heels.

Left alone, Simeon saw the utter ridiculousness in this whole situation. Why the hell did he not simply state his refusal to marry her and leave or, failing that, threaten her with the exposure of her unwise visit alone to his town house? It was the look in her eyes, he was to think later, an injured desperation that made him hesitate. The secrets were back, too, and the fear. He knew full well what people looked like when they had very little left to lose.

'Please...' She gestured, her arm visibly shaking, and because of this he followed her into a room, situated on one side of the entrance hall, that was small but tidy.

Shutting the door behind him, she leant against the portal, reminding him forcibly of their first encounter.

'I am sorry, Mr Morgan.'

Her voice was soft, uncertain, and he suddenly fancied her on the edge of tears.

'Sorry for all your lies and treachery?' He waited until she nodded. 'Take them back, then. Renounce your ridiculous inaccuracies and we shall both go our separate ways. We will never need to see each other again.'

'I can't.'

'Why?'

'Athelridge Hall is my family home. We cannot be without it.'

'I will gift it back to you, then. As soon as I return to town.'

'No.' This was said in a different tone. One far more strident. 'It is permanence I want.'

He could not believe it. He could not even consider that she might stick to such a course given his obvious dislike of her.

'You would force a marriage to take place between us that holds nothing save revulsion on my behalf? I do not wish for this union, Miss Worthington, in any form or any shape. I would pay handsomely to be rid of the hold you feel you have upon me and that will be the end of it. It is what I want. A complete and utter separation, a severance.' He could not make it plainer. 'I won't marry you under any circumstance.'

'But I think you may have to.' Her voice was quiet, edged with a kind of unbelievable certainty.

Was she mad? Was she beautiful on the outside and utterly rotten within? God, it was getting worse by the moment.

'There are rules by which all men must abide in our society, Mr Morgan, and you would lose much should you rail against them.'

'Lose what?'

He could feel his heartbeat quicken. The remnants of his recent illness, he supposed. He had been sick for over a fortnight and her lies had offered no respite from stress.

'Business relies on competence and honour. It is how the system functions.' Her voice was silken. 'Any divergence from that causes disturbance.'

'You are threatening me?'

'I do not wish to, but if I must…'

'Are you serious?' he whispered then, the incredulity in his question answered when she nodded.

'I should not impede you, Mr Morgan, in anything you might want after our marriage. I should only be a help to you. I have told you of this and once again I reiterate how much I mean to stand by such a pledge.'

At this she turned, the cloak tight around her thinness, but the door had opened and the old man he had seen before stood there, a small gun in hand.

'You need to leave. Now.'

His wrinkled hands were shaking and Simeon heard Adelia Worthington gasp even as the blaze of a bullet seared across the room, pain catching him in the side of his head.

Then he was falling. The last thing he remembered was her moving forward, her arms held out to him as if in infirmity she might finally claim him, all arguments sealed in the touch of her skin, a ragged nail raking down the top of his right hand and drawing blood.

Was he dead?

Had Cranston killed him? The old servant was speaking now, telling her something of Simeon Morgan being a threat to her and of how he was only trying to help and had not meant to touch the trigger at all. The gun lay on the floor, the smell of fresh-lit powder in the air, the seconds between horror and disbelief multiplying.

Her first finger pressed into the skin at his throat and she felt a pulse. Thready and fast.

Undoing his necktie, she laid him down, propping his feet on a pillow and loosening the buttons on his waistcoat. The wound on the top of his head was bleeding profusely and, using the cloth under the teapot to try to wipe it away, she was relieved when she saw the bullet had left only a shallow runnel in his scalp.

It had not pierced in further and there was no sign of a deadlier reality. She pushed down harder on the graze.

'He needs fresh air.' She said this as much to herself as she did to Cranston. Simeon Morgan was still, the sweat moistening his pale face easily discernible. 'Here, Cranston, you must hold this and press. The bleeding needs to stop.'

Reaching for the bell, she crossed to the window and threw open the glass, a strong northerly breeze rushing into the room. Mr Morgan would live—already his colour was returning a little and he was stirring.

Shooing her elderly servant away after finding whisky, Adelia poured a good slug of it into a crystal glass before swallowing a substantial amount herself straight from the mouth of the bottle.

She needed fortification.

If Simeon Morgan had died, that would have been the end of everything. Her father would have won.

She saw he was awake and watching her as she wiped the liquor from her mouth. Most unladylike. Barely civil. He was staring at her with such disgust she had to look away.

'You are…a drunk…like…your…father?'

'Hardly.'

His words were slurred, slightly disjointed, and the bruise on his forehead was swelling already with an alarming rapidity, dark clots of blood beneath the skin.

Then his hands were there, fending her off, trying to put a distance between them.

Adelia felt like crying. She felt like lying down beside him and simply giving up. But she could not. Instead, she slipped a plain gold ring off her own hand and placed it over his smallest finger because she could hear voices outside.

'My troth stands,' she said in the sternest voice she could manage and rose.

He was trying to sit up now, but was shaking badly. Then, having been fetched by Cranston, a groom and two Morgan men in livery filed in to give him a hand up. Simeon Morgan's vulnerability was more attractive than his bravado and she nearly blurted out a further apology, but she held it in even as he was half-carried out.

A moment later there was silence save for the quiet footsteps of Mrs Cranston.

'What will happen now, Miss Adelia?'

She shrugged her shoulders. 'I have no idea, though perhaps your husband might put his head down for the next few weeks and lie low if any strangers turn up here. If Mr Morgan wishes for retribution...' She could not finish the sentence.

The trouble was she couldn't even contemplate what to do next. Was Simeon Morgan more badly hurt than she had imagined? Would he be back with the law at his heels and revenge in his heart? Could they all be implicated in an attempted murder case? Disclosure and protections. They came in so many forms and in so many ways she was exhausted by the demands of them. Another fight? A further battle?

'You are too alone.' There was shock in Mrs Cranston's eyes at all that had transpired. 'You shoulder too much by yourself, Miss Adelia. It is not right.'

Adelia smiled, trying to reassure the woman as well as trying to steady her own racing heart.

'I am fine.'

Her hands were fastened under her cloak and she hated how they shook. Her father

would have chided her at such a weakness even
as he shouted and hit her.

But Mr Simeon Morgan had not struck out
even given such extreme provocation. He had
already passed that test. Picking up the gun at
her feet, she opened a small trapdoor built into
the foot of the far wall and dropped it inside.
Better to have no sign of the thing if Simeon
Morgan returned to accuse them. That was at
least one thing that she was sure of.

The quiet tears still falling down Mrs Cranston's cheeks shocked her, too, for the old servant was a woman who seldom cried.

Outside, she could hear a team of horses
begin to move off, the jangle of bits and stir-
rups, the turning of wheels on the stones. A
large and well-appointed conveyance fit for
a fast trip down to London. She prayed that
the motion would not kill him and the bleeding would not begin again as she grasped her
golden cross in hand.

Simeon leaned back and closed his eyes.
The movement of the carriage made him feel
ill, but so did the throb at the side of his head.
Carefully, he felt around the area, deducing

a swelling lump under his fingers, spongy and hot.

Was he going to be sick? His stomach heaved and sweat beaded on his upper lip. A small gold ring on his littlest finger glinted in the light.

'Hell.'

He fought for calm and equanimity.

Nothing was as it should have been, he thought, for when Adelia Worthington had rushed to find the whisky her cloak had fallen back and he saw she had been wearing trousers. Filthy trousers, marked with dirt and clay, her feet bootless, too-large woollen socks darned in many places.

She wanted his money. No, she needed it. It was for his fortune she had picked him out and tied a proposal to her father's near bankruptcy. His world turned.

She was like a spider setting her webs and reeling him in, stuck like prey to the strange workings of her mind. He'd seen her taking the whisky straight from the bottle when he had awoken, no small sips either, the overflow running down her chin and on to her clothes.

A drunk and crazy woman with a treacherous and dangerous beauty. A Catholic, too, for the picture of Jesus on the wall with his crown of thorns had been bedecked with a rosary.

Was there no end to her defects?

Outside he could see the traffic on the northern road building like it always did at this time of day. There were people walking, talking and laughing. A summer Wednesday, the weather warm, the sun peeping through the thinning clouds. A dog barking.

Inside, he felt frozen, motionless. He felt as though his blood had stopped running and his life had ground to a halt, incapable of thought, powerless to fashion his future in the way he wished it to go.

He shook his head and stopped. Even the slightest of movements made him dizzy and he cursed the old servant with his shaking fingers and fear. He was certain the man had not meant the thing to go off, but even knowing that was of little comfort. The house gave the impression it was only just standing and if everything was broken within it, then Miss Adelia Worthington was by far the most broken of them all.

He wished he was in bed with Teddy, the sun slanting in on their naked bodies, nothing save ecstasy and soft physical touches on the agenda. His mother's desperate marriages sat in his mind as well, both ill-mannered and ill-tempered alliances that had brought with them only disappointment and violence.

The running threads of his past unravelled. He'd been so careful in the interim years to weave the pieces of bitterness and fear into a perfect and faultless whole. No one had ever been allowed a peek into all the things he had once been and that was why marriage and its accompanying intimacies had been such a mystery to him and something he himself had never desired to experience again.

He did not want to have someone so unremittingly close to him, close enough to see gaps in the persona he presented to everyone whom he did business with. Not just business, either. In his personal relationships a void had always existed, filled with the past.

A child of the streets and a boy who was thrust into the hands of men with no care for him. A vagabond, homeless and ill fed, all the disparate patches in his clothing duplicated inside his skin.

His head ached and the thin golden ring on

his little finger seemed to draw in towards the bone, cutting off his circulation.

A day later Simeon received a letter that left him reeling. Lord Grey, an aristocrat who was interested in investing in the proposed railway outside Birmingham, had sent his congratulations on his forthcoming wedding.

Just when he'd imagined that the situation could not get any worse it had. He'd seriously thought about simply refusing Miss Worthington's ridiculous blackmail and seeing what the consequences would be, but now when the said consequences were staring him so baldly in the face it was a different story.

Money was safety to him, pure and simple, the bolster between who he had been and who he had become with graft and sacrifice and sweat and blood.

He could leave England, he supposed, simply pick up and disappear. But what of Flora Rountree? He'd been bought up lost between adults who valued neither responsibility nor honour. If he departed for the Americas, he would be subjecting the little girl to the same uncertainties that he himself had known as an eight-year-old. No home. No safety. No mercy.

No, he just could not do it. He would have to marry her, Miss Adelia Worthington, with all her faults and peculiarities, with her drunkenness and her lies and threats. There was nothing else for it. He would set up a life that was as separate as the one she had promised him, a wife without tenure save for that in name only.

The very thought made him sick, because it was exactly what his mother had done all those years ago, married his father because of her pregnancy, and look at what had happened there. She'd been a girl from a good family who had made a decision that would affect the rest of her life, a woman who could read and write and who had once loved books. His mother and father had barely had a year of marriage together before they had broken up, and whereas other women in her position might simply have admitted their error and thrown themselves back on the good will of their family, she had not. No, she had pressed on with him beside her and married again and they had fallen further and further in grace, the academic lessons he had treasured for the first ten years of his life becoming less common and food and shelter less certain. She'd been eaten up with bitter regret and rampant unhappiness, finally dying at thirty-five from syphilis, a disease that took flesh and teeth until there was very little left of her save the longing for a taste of opium pills coated in varnish and mercury.

Then his mother's uncle, James Morgan, a man of principle and learning, had found him and taken him from the streets to his own home in the north of Manchester, worlds away from the poverty and hopelessness of Angel Meadow. Without Uncle Jamie his life would have turned out so differently and Simeon had missed him terribly each and every day since his death six years ago.

God, what would have Jamie thought of him now, caught in this conundrum with Adelia Worthington and trying to make sense of it? He shook his head hard and made a decision.

There was nothing he could do save to sign the marriage contract, temper it with conditions and grin and bear it. With luck he could still live the life he was used to. He had to at least hope for that.

His first wife, Susan Downing, had been a poor choice, too. She had married him one day and he had known by the next one that their relationship was doomed. The melancholy she had hidden well was suddenly all he saw and any attempts at intimacy were met with a cloying sadness. She'd died from too much drink barely a year after they had married. At the time he'd felt only numbness, but later the guilt had settled in. A further fault in him. Another punishment.

He pulled his thoughts back to the now. The doctor had arrived yesterday afternoon and looked over the wound on his head, proclaiming both luck that he was not dead and disbelief that this whole thing had happened in the first place. Today the eye nearest the wound had darkened again, yellow and red bruises joining the blackness and swelling. He could barely see out of it.

Every person who had seen his wound had pressed him to notify the constabulary and demand redress, but the thought of the old deaf servant being thrown into prison simply for defending his mistress's honour held little satisfaction and so he'd left it. Cranston had looked absolutely petrified of retribution and the old woman behind him, presumably his wife, had been sobbing loudly.

Hell and damnation. The squalor of his early

life had been so long gone he'd thought never to see such need again and yet here it was returned in force, the headache he suffered today underlining the very guts of it all.

Crossing to the cabinet near the window, he removed a bottle and a glass and poured himself a generous drink. The doctor had said it was unwise to touch alcohol after shock, but right now he needed the sharpness taken off his pain and the aged Rémy Martin should do that nicely.

His stepbrother had died of a knife wound, caught between the anger of warring gangs. There one moment and gone the next, the lesson of impermanence and danger indelibly scored into his brain.

His mother had not even cried as she had handed him the news, instead reaching for her pills without a word and sliding into unconsciousness. It had been left to him to see Geordie blessed and buried—without any ready money, he'd needed to resort to other forms of payment.

Memories buried by necessity began to well up and he took another decent swallow of the cognac, smiling even as he did so. Perhaps he and his mother were more alike than he had thought after all, their vices different, but their methods of coping exactly the same.

Sorrow claimed him and shame followed. Like a pack of cards, his life seemed to be falling around his feet in pieces.

Chapter Three

She knew he hated her.

She knew he was furious.

She knew by every single piece of correspondence sent from his lawyers that he was fighting this sham of a betrothal with every armament in his very extensive artillery, stridently and desperately. If she was a different woman, she might have simply let him go, cut him loose, a fish on a hook that had pulled her overboard with such force she was now struggling for her own life, for air, for ever. But she was not that woman and she hadn't been for such a long time.

Oh, granted, she should never have lied about things in the first place. But after that original unsettling visit to his town house she had taken stock of her options and seen that there was, in reality, only the one.

Him.

Mr Simeon Morgan with the deeds of Athelridge Hall firmly in his pocket.

He was an outsider, a man who had grown up far from society, any family he'd had long gone. She had heard the rumours of him all Season even though he'd never once appeared at any of the glittering social events she'd attended. His money. His size. His friends who were hardly gentlemen. Society had no place to put him, no way to tag him with the labels they were so wont to do. He was a rampant and unfamiliar unknown, claiming all the spoils usually kept for the well-being of the titled aristocracy. A man no one could fathom.

A further thought crawled in to join the rest. There was safety behind the name of a man like that, there was no denying it.

'You are very quiet, Ada. Are you well?'

Her mother was walking with her on the pathways before Athelridge Hall, heavy lines marring her forehead. Adelia had made the Cranstons promise to say nothing to her of Mr Morgan's visit. She had also expressly sought their troth, not to mention his attitude to their proposed marriage and his anger directed towards it. Her mother did not need another concern on her shoulders for already she was bent over by life, a small thin woman with a constant frown on her brow.

'Adelia is quiet because she is getting married, Mama. She is thinking of her wedding probably. She is in love.'

Charlotte, her fourteen-year-old sister, turned to watch them, her face more flushed today than it had seemed yesterday. Another bout of sickness? Adelia mentally calculated the number of coins left in the family purse and frowned.

'You are pleased with this union, though, Ada?' Her mother looked at her closcly.

'Of course I am. He is a wealthy man. Besides, he alrcady owns this place. When I marry him we can stay here, Mama, for ever.'

'But is he a kind man?'

Adelia gritted her teeth. 'Very.'

'And he loves you?'

'With all of his heart.'

'It is strange that we have not met him yet. Strange he has not come here to make himself known.'

'He is busy, Mama. The railways, his enterprises...'

'Of course.'

The gown her mother wore showed up her paleness. They were all in black now, the lower windows of Athelridge Hall draped with cloth and every mirror covered.

Adelia lifted the scratchy black crepe away from the skin at her neckline, the bombazine dress she had procured hurriedly from Jay's in Regent Street an uncomfortable fit.

Full mourning at least meant that any wedding would have to be very low key. If the wedding did actually go ahead, Mr Morgan could come and then he could go away again, just as quickly. She doubted he would stay any longer than was socially expected after their last encounter even as she wondered if he would even demand consummation of such a union.

Heat drew up her body.

'I am so glad your papa knew of this, Ada, and that he approved. It makes things so much easier.' Bringing a black lace handkerchief from her pocket, she dabbed at her eyes. 'And your father's grant of Athelridge Hall as a dowry was an inspired choice because it means we should get to keep our home. Sometimes things are just so very complicated it almost makes my head ache even to think about it, but this is only simple and for that I am pleased.'

'You mustn't fret, Mama, you know worrying makes you feel unwell.' Adelia took one thin gloved hand in her own. 'Everything will be fine.'

'I know it will and our lives can go on in exactly the same way as before, thank the Lord. It does not seem like only weeks since your father passed, does it, but I suppose in the last years we did not see him much so that fact has made it a little easier to deal with.'

Adelia smiled tightly and looked away. If her mother had ever heard the gossip regarding her father's many liaisons, she had never said so.

A deaf ear. A blind eye. A fixed smile. Perhaps that was the way many women lived their lives? If she married Mr Simeon Morgan, she would be doing the very same thing for he'd made his penchant for mistresses and courtesans very plain. But his animosity still reigned supreme and she wondered if indeed he would ever capitulate.

At this point in time an absent husband did not seem so much of a sacrifice. Such a privation would allow her space to do exactly as she pleased and there were many things here that she loved.

Even as she was thinking this she caught sight of Cranston coming up the pathway towards them. When he got closer she noticed he carried an envelope.

'This has just come for you, Miss Adelia, and the man that brought it said it was to be delivered into your hands immediately. He made it very plain that it must not go astray and he is waiting as we speak in the blue salon to take the copies back.'

'Back?' She shouted this word, knowing that his hearing seemed to be deteriorating monthly.

'To the city, miss. To London.'

Adelia took the missive and opened it, but she knew exactly who it was from for the names of Simeon Morgan's lawyers were scrawled across the top.

It was a marriage contract drawn up and signed, Simeon Morgan's signature a dark scribble at the bottom. She could barely make out a single letter in the scrawl.

The Athelridge Hall estate was named as a dowry, the titles to the place included. The legal owner of the asset was Simeon Morgan, but she was a beneficial owner during her lifetime and after the death of both her and her husband the asset passed into the hands of any children resulting from their union. Other assets were also named—substantial land, estates and housing—but these were not to be placed in her name at all, but into that of any heirs that might ensue.

A measured contract. A careful agreement. There was a note attached, too, penned in the same dark writing as his signature and almost as illegible.

Miss Adelia Worthington,
Our marriage will take place in the Anglican chapel of St John's in Hyde Park Crescent on the twelfth of August at two in the afternoon.
I want as few witnesses as possible. Please include the names of those you will ask to assist you in the returning note.
Simeon Morgan

A barely hidden anger boiled from every word. A business proposition and nothing more. Could she truly do this? Could she sell her soul into bitterness and resentment?

Swallowing, she tried to look unperturbed. The wheels of her life were rolling down a pathway that could bring chaos and disaster unless she was very clever or exceptionally lucky.

'Is it the contract for your marriage, then, Ada?' Her mother at her side bent across to see the parchment.

'It is, Mama.'

'Does it say when the ceremony will take place, my dear?'

'Yes, in fact it does. It's on the twelfth of August at two in the afternoon at a chapel in Hyde Park.'

'But that's your birthday! He is a thoughtful man, then? I knew you should make a splendid marriage, my love. I knew it from the first day you were born and you were so very beautiful.'

Adelia nodded and moved away from her sister and mother.

'I will send someone back to help you and Charlotte with the vegetables you said you wanted from the garden.'

Her mother smiled. 'You are the most caring daughter that any mother could wish for.'

Cranston nodded. 'It's what my wife always says, Lady Worthington, for she has never seen a daughter so mindful of her family, which is a credit to you especially.'

Adelia swallowed down the lump that

seemed lodged in her throat and, clutching the thick envelope, she hurried up the path through the gardens towards the house.

A signature that would change Simeon Morgan's life and hers, as well. A signature that wouldn't lead to happiness, but would lead to safety.

The secrets that bound such a thought made her heartbeat quicken. She wished she were older or stronger or more powerful. She wished that her mother was less vulnerable and Charlotte less sickly, but at least that was a condition that was fixable with better food, a warmer bedroom and a doctor who would treat her more assiduously. The current lack of coin her family was cursed with meant the physician was often unavailable, his good will attached to patients who could pay more.

No, she did not need a husband who would love her and she certainly did not expect to love him back. But he did have to be strong enough to drive away the questions and she knew there were many.

The hard-hearted Adelia. The Icicle. The Snow Queen.

She had heard these nicknames attached to her. She had fought off some suitors who'd decided an approach of force was the right way of it and she had gentled others from her side after they'd sworn eternal passion from just one touch of her hand. Not one had caught her fancy with their simpering and shallow compliments.

Simeon Morgan was the only man who had ever matched her idea of strength and he was neither vindictive nor petty.

She hadn't heard a word about that devastating night at his town house whispered in any quarter. He had not exposed her. He had not abandoned her to a particular speculation when he could have so easily said the words that would have made her an outcast. Victorian society held its mores about sexual conduct close to hand after all and any woman's flagrant foolishness would never have been condoned.

Why hadn't he bared all despite her provocation? Why even with all the hate and fury present in every piece of correspondence sent had he continued to protect her from a final and disastrous public ruin? Even after being shot accidentally by her servant, he had not lain her stupidity bare.

These thoughts spun around and around as

she tucked the documents back into the envelope and went in to meet the messenger.

That evening Adelia dressed in her night-ranging clothes and went out. Past the village square, past the river and the small row of cottages that lined the street. Over the small hill behind high and rusty gates was the ancient country seat of the Thompson family. Arriving at the front door, she knocked and it was opened quickly.

Alexander Thompson stood there with a smile on his face, untidy brown hair falling around his ears.

'I thought you might come today, Ada, for I heard there was a carriage from London that had come through the village?'

'The contract came.' She did not mince her words, but gave him her news with sparseness and brevity. 'It was a reasonable one, generous even.'

'Generous to you?'

She felt the blood rise in her cheeks, a bolster against the emptiness of all that was being lost.

'If I had money...'

She shook away the words Alex did not say and moved back.

'That is not an option for us and you know it.'

'Your mother would cope if only you would let her and so would your sister because there is nothing else to do...'

She didn't allow him to finish as she moved away further.

'I know what you think and I understand what you are saying, but I cannot let my family become homeless.'

Alexander had always eschewed any responsibility, living life to the fullest in his own particular way. He had no family left now after the death of his mother two years' prior, no ties to bind him, no place that drew him back or in. He hated the house he was forced to live in and its location so far out from London town. She knew he did. But she had Mama and Charlotte to think of and, if she lost Athelridge Hall, how would they manage?

'I have made up my mind and set a plan in motion. Should I abandon it now I would never forgive myself. I swear that I would not.'

'My God, you have always been so very... virtuous. Give it a year, though, and see how you feel then, married to a man you have no reason to like. My offer stands open and there will always be a place for you here should you want it.'

Such friendship had seen her through many years of sadness and fear. Alex had been a touchstone, a sounding board, allowing her a freedom she'd found exhilarating. It was Alex who had taught her to shoot and fish and forage in the woods around the Hall. It was he who had lent her books and poems and showed her the intricacies of keeping a vegetable garden through all of the seasons and seeing it survive.

'I live on my wits, after all, and on shrewdness and if I am not a part of the world around me in the way others would want me to become, then I am all the better for it. If you could do the same, you would be much happier, but you allow others to define you, to get under your skin...'

She smiled and let him talk, about his acumen in all things concerning nature, about the foibles of others and about the common sense the world was losing with each and every consecutive year.

Adelia had heard all of this many times before and usually she agreed with everything he said, but tonight there was an empty exhaustion that filled her, a barren and hollow fatigue.

Pity.

The word came through memory and clawed in at ease.

Simeon Morgan pitied her, pitied her situation and her family, pitied her youth and her shocking offer of marriage.

He had tried again to convince her to rescind her lies by offering her a substantial sum of money through his legal representation in order to set him free. When that did not work, he had thrown in the legal deeds of Athelridge Hall as a sweetener.

A trap, she'd thought, and refused it because she could not afford to run the place, not long-term, because even a large amount of money would eventually run out. The roof on the south wing needed refurbishment and the basement under the main rooms was flooding. It was not a pittance she could manage on. Her debts were mounting by the month, worrying her as she sat with the ledgers at her desk in the middle of the night. Yet these offers had eaten at her certainty that she was doing the right thing and at the many conditions she had laid out so bluntly before him.

In all her thinking and planning she had imagined her sacrifice to be a generous one. She would have allowed him anything in truth and staying well away from her was one of those options. But now all she could see was the dishonour in it, the trick, a snare, that he did not welcome and probably had not deserved.

It was her father who had ruined things, his death nullifying the chance of ever righting the wrongs, for he'd placed his entailed estate as surety on poorly executed investment choices and a series of selfish mistakes had had disastrous consequences. If her mother had had more of a backbone, they might have managed by shifting to a smaller place and making do, but she was constantly in bed suffering from melancholy and any talk of going to live somewhere else had always been met with tears and bitter recriminations.

'What are you thinking about, Ada? Lately you have lived a life in your head that is irritating.'

Alexander's words snapped her out of her ruminations.

Irritating? Had she been more truthful she might have thrown the exact same criticism back at him, but honesty had long since been sacrificed to expedience.

'You have a small stipend which sees you through, Alex. My father has not left us even that.'

'Then why did you not find a suitor when you were in London? I told you an old, kind and forgetful one would have been the best choice. One who was not meant to be long in this world and would leave you his fortune. Surely there were some of that ilk.'

She shook her head hard. 'A woman has no say in who applies for her hand. It's a market and females are for sale. I was only a number to them, a number made more attractive given the colour of my hair and the shape of my face. God knows, I barely had a true conversation with anyone and if I tried they simply looked horrified.'

'But Morgan held the deeds to Athelridge Hall and so he was chosen?'

'It was a large plus in his favour to be sure.'

'He sounds too virile, too masculine. He sounds untameable.'

At that she almost laughed.

'Before I travelled to London I had not thought power an important attribute, but perhaps it is the only thing I do need now.'

'I disagree. If you cannot wrap Morgan around your little finger, how do you see your marriage proceeding?'

She was glad at that moment that Alex was not a party to all she had promised Simeon Morgan.

'With caution,' she replied and turned away.

'We should have married, Adelia, and damn the consequences. We still can, if you are game? It would be some kind of a protection for you.'

The words fell into the space between them.

Once she might have said yes, but now... Over the past few years she had seen a change in Alexander, a bitterness that kept on rising. He blamed everyone for his own situation and the constant stream of criticism had begun to be wearying. Sometimes she even wondered if he was quite sane.

The younger version of herself had thought him more dashing than she did now. Granted, he was handsome and he read widely. But his compassion for others had dulled whereas hers had sharpened, the plight of her family leading her now with much more force.

London had also changed her and for the first time ever she felt that beauty might not be quite the asset everyone around her had always painted it to be. Her mother, her father, Alexander, the suitors.

Simeon Morgan had not mentioned her looks once and had never complimented her. He wasn't thunderstruck by her dimples or by the way she had spoken. Even the colour of her hair, which more normally seemed to drive sensible men into raptures, had hardly signified.

No, he had looked inside her and judged her lacking. Her own doubts also had begun to surface. There were other young women there in the salons of society who had been plain but bold, interesting women of conversation and ideas. Perhaps her looks had reduced her to something less, something diminished in his eyes.

She had shifted sideways somehow, out of balance with her life as she had always known it.

The sheer wonderment of Simeon Morgan's caresses was a part of everything, too, her body melting into warmth as she remembered that night. Was that unusual? Was it normal to feel so very heated when a man did those things?

She had no experience in such matters, no yardstick to measure anything by.

Oh, granted, Alex had kissed her a few times when they were younger and she had liked it, but the feelings she'd once had for him had paled and weakened. Now when she looked at him she saw a man who held no real place in the world and had no true understanding of it.

A surprising honesty, that, given how for years she had followed him about like a puppy dog, hoping and praying that he would give her his heart.

Everything was skewed. She was her family's keeper now and if she failed at the responsibility...

When Alex suddenly reached out and pulled her to him and his lips came down across her own all she felt was shock. He was cold and his teeth hurt. He smelled of strong liquor, too, as he ground away at her mouth. A misguided intimacy. When his hand strayed to her breast she pushed it away and was glad when he let her go.

'I'm sorry.' His voice shook. 'I thought…'

She smiled, trying for all she was worth to replace an ease back where only awkwardness now lingered.

'It's been a long day, Alexander, and I am tired.'

Tired to death, she almost said. Tired to death of making everything all right for everyone else. Tired of pretence and deceit and tired of hope, as well; the hope that all her problems would somehow resolve into a future that could be liveable.

Simeon Morgan's caresses were there, too, the attention he had given her, casually, with barely a shred of importance. A thrown-off intimacy. A pity. An unconcerned insouciance that bordered on indifference.

She had been caught in a web of lies that had tethered themselves around her and would not let go.

'You need to start thinking of yourself, Adelia. You have to understand that your family is pulling you down into mediocrity. You must leave them behind and begin a new life. You are getting older and life is beginning to play on your face in a way that is not attractive.'

Alexander's words hurt, but she merely nodded and left, closing the door between them with a quietness belying her anger. She had no energy left to make him understand who she was now and what she had to do.

Outside she slipped into the shadows of trees, skirting around moonlight and listening to the night sounds as she walked. There was barely a wind and the rain held off. She felt the damp, skin-close, a front coming down across the northern hills, a ring of hazy silver around the moon.

Her place. Known and dear, the sounds, the smells, the feel of the earth under her feet and the vision of the wide-open sky above. The lump in her throat thickened, but she shook it away. Now was not the time for fear. She couldn't afford it, for one thing, and, for another, if she started crying she wondered if she might ever stop.

Icy Adelia. Cold Adelia. Unfeeling Adelia.

The names others called her haunted her memory. Her father had made her such. But so had her mama with all her neediness and unworldliness, a woman of small opinions and anxious understanding.

Tonight she had seen the same lack of care in Alexander's selfishness, too, his ego resting on a greed that had not been apparent to her before.

Alone.

Lonely.

Lost.

Pitiful.

That last word just would not leave her, even here in the dark quiet of night, and in a place where she had always found solace. In two weeks she would be married to a man who hated her, but because of that union Athelridge Hall would be hers for ever. For as long as she lived. For as long as her family needed shelter.

It was enough.

It simply had to be.

She bit down on terror and made for home.

Chapter Four

St John's Chapel, Hyde Park Crescent
August 12th

Simeon Morgan was waiting. There was fury in the taut slant of his lips, though he turned only briefly to look at her before he stood ramrod straight again at the head of the aisle, a stillness in him that was worrying.

Like a snake about to strike.

There were so few people here and the dress Adelia wore felt suddenly and horribly out of place. A lacy white-silk affair with embossed flowers and seed pearls. Her mother had insisted on it even in their state of mourning. It had been her own when she had married and they had altered it so it was now a more fashionable style.

If it had been left to Adelia, she'd have gone to the altar in her black bombazine edged in scratchy crepe. A penance. A sacrament. The colour underlining all she now felt inside. Dead. Numb. Disbelieving.

Her small family sat bolt upright in the front left pew, Simeon Morgan's two guests occupying the front right.

A man and a woman.

The man was tall and austere, the woman gowned in a deep green velvet, a colour that matched her wild red hair. Two large pale breasts were displayed prominently.

No one spoke.

She could hear light rain on the roof above them, the wind behind it in a rush. At the altar was a single bunch of white lilies in a vase dressed with greenery, the only part of the whole ceremony that was normal and expected. She wondered who had provided them. The minister's wife, perhaps, or the ladies of the parish? Some gentle woman who had noticed the lack of ornamentation and remedied it?

She chanced a look at her reluctant groom. He appeared bigger today. He looked healthier, too, though the glint in his golden eyes was flat and indifferent. He could have been standing in line at the theatre or waiting to be served at the bar of some tavern so little emotion did he display.

She heard Charlotte draw in breath and sniff, the sound echoing around the holy room. She was getting yet another cough. Adelia wished the ceremony might begin as it was cold in here and all she wanted was for everything to be over.

Her mother sat beside Charlotte, her face drawn and a worried look in her eyes. The sum total of her family.

It had begun to pour now in earnest, the drizzle of the day finally deciding to mean something.

'Miss Worthington?' The query made her start, her attention regathered. The minister stood before her, smelling of wine and peppermints, his fingernails clean and long. 'If you could come forward now with Mr Morgan, we are ready to begin.'

So this was it then. Four guests, each looking more bewildered than the next one. Certainly her mother was gesturing her over as though she wished to have a word, but Adelia simply shook her head and stepped forward to the altar to stand by her groom, a stranger with his long dark hair and eyes of burning golden amber.

It was done.

Finished.

This was the very best that she could manage to save her family and the only alternative that might work if she was lucky.

She didn't look at Simeon Morgan because at that moment she wanted to believe that he was there as a protection. Against herself and all the secrets that lay hidden inside, stopping her from being whole.

The hand closest to her was balled into a fist, every knuckle white. He wore a single ring on his little finger, a ring of gold encrusted with stones of silver.

A ring?

She had not thought of providing one in all the chaos and uncertainty. She had not thought to procure a bauble that might signify for ever because she knew he would not want it. She wondered what had happened to the plain gold ring she had stuck on his finger after Cranston's bullet had almost killed him.

The minister's voice was deep and very clear.

The grace of our Lord Jesus Christ,
the love of God,
and the fellowship of the Holy Spirit
be with you...

'Be with you...'

She found herself replying as he went on into the preface and then the declarations. Words of grace and hope and beauty. Words that she had long since given up on and thrown away, the empty and flat optimism holding no promise at all.

She knew her groom felt the same as he shuffled suddenly, his highly polished shoes reflecting the light under well-creased trousers. Two people standing in a charade that the Lord above must surely decry. When the rain became heavier again she wondered if it was not a sign of displeasure that fell from the heavens on to the little Anglican chapel of St John's in Hyde Park Crescent on the afternoon of her twentieth birthday.

Stop this deception. Repent of your sins.

She could almost hear the voice of an omnipotent God, warning her, warning him.

But behind on the first pew Charlotte, who was normally more morose, was taking an interest. The ghost of her father was here, too, the bitterness Lionel Worthington harboured diminished somehow by the mellow religious overtones.

Her family would survive if she went through with this and might even flourish. The hope of it kept Adelia still as she listened to the curate. Words of sickness and health, words of honour and promise till death do us part. Words of permanence and grace and glory.

Then it was over. She was married. For better or for worse. She had thought Simeon Morgan might have choked on such promises, but he had said the words without faltering, a surprising strength in each declaration. In truth, he had managed the vows with more aplomb than she had.

Her ring was beautiful, fashioned from rose gold with stones of emerald. There was no show in it at all, none of the excess that was so apparent in his house. It was simply plain and tasteful.

He'd supplied his own ring himself, a thick gold band. Perhaps he'd had the bauble already and did not wish to procure another for it did not appear to be new, the burnished metal aged under light.

When he had placed the emerald ring on her finger his hands had been warm, but when she looked up at him he had not met her glance. It was as if, once the protocols had been observed, he had distanced himself. She could feel this in his stance and in the way he half-turned from the altar, the kiss that usually took place after the final troths refused summarily.

The two guests on his side of the church had come to stand next to him and both were looking her way.

Simeon Morgan's demeanour changed as the beautiful red-haired woman took his arm, her hand tucked into the crook of his elbow in a manner that announced she knew him well.

Not a sister, but a lover, one of the mistresses he had told her of probably, thrust into her face during the very hour of their union.

'You will have broken a thousand hearts, Sim, by going through with this. I hope you realise just how lucky you are, Miss Worthington?'

Adelia had no idea at all how to answer such a provocative statement and so she stayed silent, noting that the other woman had refused to address her by her married name.

* * *

Simeon felt Adelia's displeasure at Theodora's words. He should not have brought his mistress to his wedding ceremony, but he'd done it in a fit of pique. He made no attempt to remove Teddy's arm from his either, allowing the contact to remain even under the frown of Tom Brady's notice. The haughty distance of his new wife was something he well remembered from his past and he did not mean to bend to it on this occasion or any other.

She was cossetted, aristocratic, conceited. If he was honest with himself, though, she had also looked frightened today, her small thin paleness magnified against the white of her gown. At her throat the gold cross glinted and he saw how her fingers kept returning to it time after time, seeking guidance, perhaps, or praying for a miracle?

Her fingernails were neither painted nor long, the short clean shape of them appealing as she clutched her simple bouquet of cut white roses close. Her hair was swept upwards, tiny tendrils of differing shades of blonde escaping the strictures and curling about her face. He frowned at the dimples furrowing each cheek.

If she had looked beautiful all the other

times he had seen her, then this occasion magnified even those. He'd noticed the surprise in Tom's eyes as she had entered the chapel and also seen the short flare of jealousy in Teddy's.

His new bride had the power to divide people, he thought suddenly, for, like all beautiful women, he was certain she would know the strength of her assets and use them accordingly.

A book was brought forward, a register of marriages in the small chapel of St John's, the religious traditions of hundreds of years imbued in its pages.

The newest entry looked like an impostor.

Her name was Adelia Hermione Josephine Bennett Worthington. It was her birthday today, he saw, and a small pang of guilt pierced his heart.

Her writing was well formed and carefully controlled, though her hand shook as she placed her name in the space provided. When she passed him the quill he saw she was careful not to touch his hand and for that he was grateful.

She smelt like a country garden. She smelt of sunshine. Around her head she had a garland of white floral jasmine, threaded with fragile greenery and thin ribbon. Her dress was plain but pretty. The stitches at her bodice gave the impression of a gown that had been refashioned. It certainly looked nothing like those the women of London's society more normally wore.

He wondered what might happen if he simply reached out and grabbed her hand and commanded that there should be no more lies between them. Could taking such a risk glue all the cracks that had appeared so quickly?

Folly, he then thought, and stupidity. In this dress in front of her family and in a church that was so plainly not her own she was only pretending an innocence, a meekness she did not possess. There could be no other explanation.

Blessed are the meek, for they shall inherit the earth.

The passage from Matthew suddenly came to mind.

What was it to be meek? He knew many assumed the term to mean tame or deficient in courage, but the years he had lived with his uncle had whipped up a different understanding, for Jamie Morgan's meekness had been that of power under control.

She lifted her head to look at him just as

he did the same and the glance between them caught as flame. Not easy. Not expected either, but a burning, scorching, blistering blaze that reduced those all around them to mere ashen shadow.

His heartbeat quickened and the core of his body warmed. What the hell had just happened? Was Adelia Worthington a sorceress, a conjurer who might bewitch him if everything else she had tried should fail?

Not Worthington now, either, but Morgan. Mrs Adelia Morgan. The name rang in his mind like music and that worried him, too.

Blood rushed across her face in waves and Adelia tipped her head down, making much of reading the lines in the register before her, but she was really trying to regain a sense of normality. Mr Morgan had looked at her as if he might simply eat her up in one lustful bite, leaving nothing but bleached bones behind in a small discarded pile. And the ridiculous thing was she would have followed him anywhere he led her just to know that which she saw promised in his face.

Tonight?

That one word hovered around her. Would

he stay with her? Would he demand his rights as a husband? Would he undress her under candlelight slowly and carefully and show her all the things he had started to in London when first she had visited him?

Her breasts tightened under the whiteness of the gown so that her nipples stood up proud against the thin silk. A sacrifice for her family. A ransom for her father's sins. A wife who knew she would never hold any place at all in her new husband's heart. A daughter who had seen things no daughter ever should.

That thought had her sucking in a breath and she looked at the stained-glass window above showing a picture of the crucified Jesus. Not here, she thought, not here in this place of the eternal God and Jesus and the Holy Ghost.

The tall man who had come as Simeon Morgan's guest signed the register as a witness and then her mother followed. Adelia was glad that the red-headed woman had returned to her seat, for there was something in her look that told Adelia much more than she wished to know.

The man whose name was Thomas Brady according to his signature smiled at her and she smiled back. A simple gesture of friendship in a landscape of hidden meanings and danger. She wished it was all over.

And then suddenly it was. There would be no wedding breakfast, no speeches, nothing more to cement the union. She watched as her new husband left, simply taking the arm of the handsome woman he had arrived with and walking back down the aisle. He was followed out by his tall friend.

Their carriage stood on the roadway and amid lively chatter they entered the conveyance and were gone, a rush of hooves, the cry of the driver, the rain swallowing them up before they had gone a hundred yards.

The minister observed her, uncertainty staining his expression and her mother frowned, thin hands turning a handkerchief this way and that as she spoke.

'Is he gone? How are we to get home?'

Adelia turned to look at her sister staring at her.

'There has been a misunderstanding, I am afraid.' She screwed the emerald ring off her finger and held it out to the minister before her.

'Could I ask you to lend me a few pounds under the surety of this ring, sir?'

The man of God looked rattled.

'Just until I can come back to claim it and return your kindness.' She bowed her head as he hesitated and lifted the gold cross from around her neck as an added inducement. 'Our Lord in all his wisdom and grace would surely wish for you to help a family in need.'

'Indeed, Mrs Morgan, indeed.'

He rifled through his generous pockets and produced three golden coins.

'Will this be enough for your needs?'

'It will,' she replied, 'and I thank you.'

Once outside Adelia walked in the rain across four busy wet roads to find a hackney in her thin white dress with the flowers in her hair. The bouquet she gifted to a washerwoman who offered her direction and if she felt eyes upon her as she hurried by, she ignored them.

It was done and she deserved such a penance. It was finished and this was to be her punishment, left in the bridal chapel to find her own way home, left to the wits she had about her to see her family safe.

When a conveyance was procured she jumped aboard and sat down on cushioned leather, unmindful of the small puddle of wet coldness that was pooling around her.

In another two moments they were outside the chapel and her mother and sibling tumbled in.

'You lied to us, Adelia.' These were her mother's first words. 'I think your husband hates you.'

'Better hatred than homelessness,' she replied and wiped the mucus from Charlotte's running nose with the back of her cold hand.

Her mother laughed at that, a sound so unexpected that Adelia could only stare.

'You are exactly your father's daughter,' she said as the horses moved off.

'I sincerely hope not.' She bit at the soft flesh on the inside of her mouth to stop herself from saying more.

Simeon dropped off Theodora under protest of his not coming in and spending the night with her. Unwinding her hands from around his neck, he tried to be gentle, shifting her weight from leaning upon him, dodging the kisses that she insisted on bestowing. Once back in the carriage he also had Tom to contend with.

'Your wife might wonder where you are, Sim.'

'I doubt it.'

'I personally had expected at least a bite to eat.'

Simeon laughed. 'There is a pub around the corner that serves a good meal. We will go there and you can choose whatever you like.'

'Your bride didn't really have the look of a harridan.'

'Pardon?'

'A harridan. An ice queen. A harpy. All the things that were said about her in society. I thought she seemed afraid more than anything and Theodora Wainwright was hardly making things easier.'

'She knows I keep mistresses,' Simeon pointed out grimly.

'Well, more normally it is at a distance, surely?'

The truth of this was worrying him, but he could not afford to feel guilty. She had tricked him into this whole ridiculous debacle after all.

'Usually marriages of convenience have a modicum of civility. I am afraid to say, Tom, that mine does not. But I have been generous in the contracts and that, after all, was what Adelia Worthington wanted the most.'

'Adelia Morgan now, Sim. Though perhaps

that may not signify if you don't mean to consummate the union.'

Simeon frowned. 'Oh, I most heartily do
not. Non-consummation of this farce of a marriage could be my only way to dissolving such
nonsense at a later and more private date. But
right now I need to go and get stinking drunk.
A few hours of oblivion are exactly what is
called for and I mean to find them.'

Back in Athelridge Hall Adelia shut the door
and stood there, silent, unmoving, feeling the
terror shift a little, feeling the embarrassment
finally dislodge.

She had brought them home, her mother
helped up to bed by the ageing Mrs Cranston.
Charlotte had stomped off without speaking
apart from the usual tirade about hating her
family.

Tonight with all her own concerns piling up
Adelia took little mind of her younger sister's
anger and instead ordered everyone a plate of
hot food from the kitchens and went to her
own room.

The wedding dress was indelibly stained
now. From the mud on the road, from the
rain, from Charlotte's streaming nose and her

mother's thickly applied powder where she had slept fitfully against her shoulder on the drive home.

She peeled it off, the petticoats beneath following, and was pleased to have the rudiments of the day gone. The flowers in her hair she was more careful with for she had spent a good deal of time in the making of the small embellishment. She laid them on her side table, arranging the ribbons in soft tailed streams. The silk boots of her grandmother were ruined. She could do nothing for them save throw them in a corner to be dealt with in the morning.

Then all that was left was her, pale in the candlelight. An unwanted wife. A nuisance. She thought for a moment she might lie down on her bed and cry, but shook her head hard at such cowardice.

Was Simeon Morgan at this very moment laughing with his red-haired mistress at the ridiculous farce of their union? She'd seen the woman cuddling up to him in the carriage as it had left, glued to his side with a close familiarity.

Her own future looked bleak.

If they did not consummate the marriage, her foothold here at Athelridge Hall was far less certain. Just once would be enough. Once to make the vows legal and binding and permanent. And if she got with child then all the better, for the whole world would understand her tenure at the Hall rather than joining her husband in London and the gossip might stop.

A knock at the door had her reaching for a blanket and securing it about her. Mrs Cranston came in with hot potato soup and fresh bread smothered in salty butter.

'I had not expected you all back quite so soon, Miss Adelia, and your mother is having a fit of crying for all she is worth. I take it the wedding was not a success?'

'Perhaps not, but it is done now. I am the new Mrs Morgan.'

'And do you think it was worth it?'

'I hope so.'

'You are braver than anyone I know and you have always made the best of a bad situation. I pray that your new husband realises what a treasure he has had the luck to find and is repentant.'

'That, Mrs Cranston, is very doubtful, but at least from now on there will be food enough on our table.'

'And you won't be off so much hunting and gathering. Well, that is a relief.' She stopped for a moment, measuring her words. 'Would he hit you, Miss Adelia, in anger? Like your father did?'

'I think not.'

'Then you are indeed lucky. Food on the table and an even temper. There are many women who have far less than that.'

'Mrs Cranston?'

'Yes.'

'Go to bed early tonight. No one will need you for we are all exhausted.'

A wide smile was returned.

'I shall, my dear, and Mr Cranston shall retire with me after seeing to the doors and the windows.'

When she was gone Adelia found her old shift and pulled it on, layering a woollen shawl over the linen. There was no fire laid so she tumbled into bed, pulling the quilt across her and leaning back on the pillows she had stuffed last year with goose down. The day had made her feel frozen.

She no longer had the ring or her cross, but she held the words of the ceremony in her memory and turned them over in her head.

Troths of hope and love and honour. Empty promises, faithless pledges. Gulping down the soup, she ate the bread, dampening her finger to retrieve the very last delicious crumbs off the plate. Tomorrow was another day and she meant to use it wisely.

The tomatoes had to be picked and there was a row of onions standing near the kitchen door to be threaded. The three cows needed milking, the eggs needed to be collected and the grass by the main gate needed to be scythed. And those were only the jobs requiring finishing in the first part of the morning.

She would need to retrieve her ring and cross, too, of course, but lacking the coin to pay the minister back right now, she meant to leave the jewellery there for a week or two. Surely he would keep them safe for her. Surely he would not pawn them to retrieve so few pounds before she had a chance to see to it herself.

It was her birthday today and no one had remembered.

Twenty.

A woman now.

Reaching for her rosary, she said a quick night prayer before laying the beads back under her pillow. She missed her cross, the piece of jewellery she had inherited from her maternal grandmother when she was born and had always worn. She missed it far more than the expensive new ring Simeon Morgan had placed on her hand while reciting promises that meant nothing to him.

The day tumbled across her mind even as the rain outside lulled her into sleep.

It was full black when she awoke, coming into consciousness with a startle. Someone was in the house, she was sure of it, poised on the first-floor landing with the creaky board underfoot. It would not be her mother, for she was afraid of the dark. It would not be her sister, either, for the day had worn them both out.

The servants had gone to bed—she had heard them leave herself. The Cranston annexe was at the back of the house.

Sitting up, she listened, tilting her head in the direction of the door. When she heard another creak, she struck a light to her candle and rose, grabbing her shawl in one hand and the heavy brass fire poker in the other.

Her handle turned slowly and she waited. Then the door was pushed open and she knew immediately just who her unexpected intruder was.

'You.' She could not disguise her relief. Not

a burglar, after all, out to do her harm, but her new husband, his hair wet from the rain and the substantial cloak draped around his shoulders damp.

He blinked, trying to focus, the red in his eyes telling her he was more than inebriated and that it would not be long before he was also unconscious.

'Needed to...see you, Adelia.'

The words were whispered.

'Needed...to tell...you something. Forgot.'

One finger came to his lips and he held it there, signalling quiet.

'How did you know this was my room?'

He frowned. 'I asked your...sister. She was...downstairs.'

'Charlotte?'

'Is that her...name? Didn't know it. Looked... a bit...sad.'

She should push him out. She should knock him over the head with the poker for the embarrassment of leaving her in the lurch at the chapel in Hyde Park Crescent. She should do both those things, but another thought also struck her.

She could use this situation to her advantage. It was like a good fortune falling unexpectedly into her lap, her first stroke of luck in years.

Consummation.

Pouring him a liberal glass of her father's whisky, she handed it over, pleased when he took it. The bottle had been brought up a few weeks ago when she had caught a cough and had not been returned to the library downstairs.

'Sit down.' She gestured to the chair by her bed and he did as she bade him, tucking the folds of his cloak around himself as he smiled.

'Your house is...different here. The colours...suit you.'

She looked around, seeing the soft shades she had chosen to decorate. Faded yellows, mellow creams. A bolt of light blue fabric she had found in the attic, a leftover from better bygone days.

The candlelight suited him, too. He looked younger tonight. The gold in his eyes was the same shade as the whisky in his glass, fired by light.

'How did you get here?'

'Hackney. Hired one.'

'All the way from London at this time of night?'

He frowned as if his sense was returning and he could not quite believe where he was.

'Not right...to just leave you... Should have...seen you home.'

His hand came out and before she could move he had hers in his grasp, turning it over to trace the lines with a finger. 'My mam... read palms for a living and...she was good at it.'

He stopped and she saw the pain in his expression. His skin was warm and his fingers long.

'She said everyone's future lies in their past. I...used to hope...not.'

His rough accent was much more pronounced tonight, the burr of the long drawn-out vowels, the rolling r's and the missed h's as well as his use of the word 'mam'. It was the drink, she supposed. Every other time she had met him his words had been more clipped and careful, a melded accent of time and distance.

'Why did you come here?'

'It's your...birthday.'

He let her go then and dug into a pocket bringing out a burnished brown-velvet box. 'A present to match the ring.'

Depositing it on the table, he held on to the

edge for balance and she wondered if he felt dizzy even as her heart warmed at his gift. He had seen her birthdate on the marriage certificate, no doubt.

'I want things to be…civil…between us. Only that… Was married once before…a long time ago and never wanted to be again…'

Shock ran through her. 'What happened to your wife?'

'She died.' He didn't say more, his big frame leaning in a graceful arc back against the chair.

'Know the difference, though…between right and wrong. So many things are wrong. Wrong to leave you there…with a sick sister… in the rain on your birthday. Wrong to bring Teddy to the wedding…'

He'd closed his eyes now, momentarily, a weariness on his face that pulled at her compassion. Simeon Morgan was drunk, but kind with it, and he was not a bully.

It was enough.

Lord, thought Adelia, could it actually be this easy?

'She is not…usually…nasty. Just…jealous. Needed to tell you before…' He stopped and looked around as if seeing the room for the first time. The smell of drink on his breath was strong.

'Before what?'

'Before you went to sleep…on your birthday.'

'Stand up.' She didn't waste words and was glad he did as she asked. His height was emphasised here in her room in the eaves of the roof, a tall man with muscles that none of the lords in society seemed to sport. In this light she noticed a white scar across his left cheek near his eye.

When he saw where she looked one finger rose to touch it. 'Wasn't fast enough…sometimes.'

His smile was lopsided and nearly broke her heart, the child he had been who must have tried to dodge such violence suddenly conjured up.

He was swaying, too, as she unbuttoned his cloak and then his jacket and threw them on to a nearby chair. The waistcoat beneath was one of embossed satin.

'Too many…clothes. You, too.'

His glance was on the bed now and she saw desire flare in his eyes, an under-shade of brown in the amber. His fingers touched the straps of her linen nightgown, pulling one side off her shoulders.

'Want you, Adelia.'

'Sit down, then.' She patted the bed and he almost fell upon it.

Kneeling, she unbuckled his polished leather shoes, the silver buckles engraved with his initials. Then she removed his necktie as he watched her every move. Like an indolent male lion, power and strength harnessed, but undeniably there.

Her breath caught and held. It was a dangerous game that she played and one which might go either way. If he was not quite drunk enough…

He lay back even before she asked him to do so, lifting his legs from the floor and closing his eyes.

'Drunk…too…much. Damn it. Shouldn't have.' His breathing evened out into a quiet snore, the sound reassuring.

With care she removed her shawl, not sufficiently daring to take off her linen shift as well, and climbed in behind him, pulling the quilt across the both of them.

Eleven o'clock.

With luck Mrs Cranston would come in to

wake her at six. That gave him seven hours
to sober up, seven hours to realise just what
boundaries had been crossed, seven hours to
understand that the wife he had left at the altar
in the small chapel on the edge of Hyde Park
was now undeniably his. To have and to hold
for ever. A solemn and unbreakable vow.

Moving her arm a little, she held her breath
as her touch came up against him, the warmth
comforting. He did not flinch and so she left it
there, the experience of having someone share
her bed for the first time in her life strangely
joyful. He was not like any of the swains that
she had met across her Season. He had never
mentioned her looks and he certainly had made
no real advances towards her, save in that ridiculous first meeting when she had confronted
him with her proposal.

If she closed her eyes and sought the memory, everything was still so vivid. In all honesty she wished he might awake now and touch
her again exactly as he had before. Tipping her
head, she hid a smile, his waistcoat against her
cheek smooth and silken. She hoped he would
not be too hot in such a garment, though the
night was cool, the cold spell breaking any

summer heat and returning the temperatures of spring to early August.

She could smell the alcohol on him under the musky scent of manhood. He did not use cologne or any perfumes. Smoke lay in the fibre of his clothes and she wondered where he had been since they had left each other in Hyde Park at three.

She sniffed again. The flame-haired sultry beauty he had brought to her wedding had reeked of some exotic scent, but that was gone. His arm moved suddenly as he turned and came against her, one hand cupping her shoulder.

She lay deathly still and waited, but his breathing settled again and his profile softened. In the moonlight his hair curled around his ears and was much longer than most men in society wore theirs. He had thick eyelashes and his cheeks were chiselled high. His nose held a break on the bridge, she was sure of it, a relic of his life as a boy, she supposed, given the rumours that were threaded around him.

A self-made man, a man who would confound all expectations. The thick gold wedding band on his fourth finger glinted in the light.

Her husband.

She wished he had come to her bed willingly. She wondered what might happen tomorrow when he realised her trick. She prayed he might wake and turn in the dark to hold her, like he had the first time they met. She wanted the heat from him to seep into her bones and words that were loving to fall from his lips.

An owl called outside, through the night. It was late and today had been exhausting. Yet she lay listening to his breathing and feeling his hand across her until sleep finally took her down into the dark quiet.

Chapter Five

For a moment Simeon wondered just where he was. A strange room. A quilt pulled up across him. The light filtered through pale blue curtains, birdsong and sunshine.

He felt the warmth behind him like a shock, snuggled in, one small hand tucked across him, pale hair flowing in a tangle of curls, a scent of lemon and flowers and woman.

The old servant woman was standing there in the doorway, her mouth open, and when she cried out the cup she had been carrying fell, the hot and scalding tea leaving small plumes of steam rising as it ran into the gaps between the floorboards.

Adelia had scrambled up now from behind him, her shift low across her bosom, her legs bare. The bruises he had seen the night she'd first visited were faded now, only a small shadow of them behind her neck remaining.

Oh, hell. Had he slept with her here at Athelridge Hall on the night of their union? How on earth had he got here? The last he remembered he was in a tavern at the end of Regent Street in the company of Tom Brady and a dozen other men they knew. Drinking as quickly as he could and trying to drown his sorrows.

His wedding night.

Consummation?

Had he hurt her? Had he been rough? The fragments of worried questions piled in, each one barely thought of before another took its place.

Some of his clothes were still on him at least. His waistcoat, shirt and trousers. Even his belt was buckled at the waist.

Not that, then? But what?

The thin pale mother was there now, too, her mouth also wide-open, but without words. Like a play he had seen in a theatre in Covent Garden, a comedy, a tragedy, a satire. No end to the misunderstandings.

Adelia was shooing them out, shutting the door behind them and locking it. He saw the deep breath she took before she turned.

'It can't be undone now, this marriage of ours.' There was fire in her eyes.

'But I didn't...' He stopped, knowing that it would make no difference now there were witnesses.

The silence stretched out, a raft of questions, a slew of uncertainties. He could think of absolutely nothing he might say so he simply watched while she took her shawl and wrapped it around her, the tight cocoon of light blue wool hiding any hint of skin whatsoever.

'My God, I cannot believe this.' The blasphemy fell into the growing silence, making her wince. 'How did you get home from the chapel?'

'I pawned your ring and my necklace. The minister drove a hard bargain.'

Her answer was so unexpected he hardly knew what to say. Every time he had seen her she looked different. This morning he could see how young she truly was and he felt at that second every one of his own twenty-seven years.

'Where do we go from here?' His words came without thought.

'You go on with your life and I go on with mine. I promised you that you were free to do just as you wanted and I meant it.'

He laughed, though the sound held no humour for he knew that his old life was gone. Adelia Worthington was not the bride he would have chosen, but right now she was playing by the rules. She had not reneged on the things she had promised him and for that at least he was grateful. It seemed it might be possible to leave her here, away from his own life, away from wifely demands and needs and tantrums.

If he played this right, he might not have to be bothered with her again and yet in that thought he felt some sort of regret. The vestiges of Holy Matrimony, he presumed, or the calm after the storm. Her hair fell almost to her waist in a curling mass of wheat and gold and white.

'Why did you have so many bruises on your arms when first I met you?'

Fright kept her still and a defensiveness that he had not seen in her before rose, closing down her face.

'You do not need to worry about me, Mr Morgan. I am fine.'

'Fine to live in a house that looks as though it might fall about your knees? Fine to sleep in a bed with a hole in the roof above it?'

She didn't answer.

'I will send one of my bookkeepers to take a look around. Once he understands the basic needs here we can form a monthly budget.'

He watched as she sat down hard upon a chair by the window, hands on each side as though she was shocked. She was so thin she looked like a large gust of wind might simply knock her over.

'Food. Clothing. Heating. That sort of thing. Medicine if your sister needs it. She does not look well.'

Adelia felt her head spinning, every one of his words like an answer to a prayer. He would help them? He would not abandon her to the trials of impending poverty even given her deceit?

He was standing now, reaching for his boots and slipping them on, his other clothing laid across his arm as though he would carry them. In the light she could see the quality of everything he wore, the cut of the excellent fabric and the expertise of every stitch. His wedding clothes were rumpled, but still beautiful. Hers, on the other hand, had had one wear too many.

She noticed another scar across his right hand running from the base of the thumb completely over the top to his little finger.

'Simeon Morgan was brought up hard.'

She had heard that said of him many times at the balls. His name had come up often at such events because most of the girls and their mothers hoped he might attend. Money, she supposed, paved the way for anything and it was whispered loudly that he had a fortune. Her own lack of it was one of the reasons they had had to make a dash from London. Although she had told her mother she had paid all their outstanding bills, in truth she had not been able to. Should she say something about that now?

She decided not to, for the détente they shared was too fragile to be broken. Perhaps she might mention it to the bookkeeper he spoke of when he came. If he came.

'Do you keep horses here?'

She nodded. 'One. A stallion.'

'Would he get me to London, do you think?'

'I doubt it, but the village would be within his range if you rode him very slowly.'

'And I could find another steed there?'

'Certainly. The Stanley Stables would happily provide you with a transport back to town.'

She saw him look around the room, at the ring of flowers wilted now on the side table and at her wedding dress hung on the front of the wardrobe, dirty and still damp. She was glad the boots were out of sight because even she could tell they would never be the same.

'It seems a long time since yesterday,' he said and she knew exactly what he meant. Everything from their wedding was spoiled or missing, rumpled or wilted.

Without pause, she decided to throw another of her secrets into the mix.

'My mother is an ardent Catholic and I have taken up some of her beliefs.'

'I know. I saw a rosary dangling on the picture downstairs and there is another one beneath your pillow.'

'Mama is most devout for religion is her great crutch. I tell you this because surprise is often unwelcome, I find, and it is always better to have formed some plan as to how you might react before the truth can stun you.'

'Is that how you have managed so far?'

'I played it a little false when I told you I was an unmitigated success in society. At first that was true, I suppose, but after a while… I wasn't.'

'Why not?'

'I couldn't understand what it was they wanted from me. When Mr Anstruther pushed me up against a tree in Hyde Park and tried to fondle my breasts I had had enough. I hit him with my umbrella and he fell over. It was just unlucky his head struck the tree trunk as he went down.'

'What happened next?'

'His mother and her friend came at my calls and both blamed me. They said I was a tease. They asked me to leave and so I did, though later I heard it said I had deserted a wounded man in the park and had made no effort to help him. My character was deemed to be a selfish one with little to recommend it and the swains drifted off. I was glad for it, but my father was not.'

'He wanted you married?'

'Like any father would, I expect.'

Something had changed as soon as her father was mentioned. Simeon knew it by her tone as she turned away, her hand pushing back her hair. As a child he had become so adept at recognising untruths he was always surprised when others seemed to have no notion of it.

He wished they could go back to where they were a moment ago, having a conversation that was not forced or unnatural. Adelia was beautiful when she was being honest.

'He was a man I disliked, your father. He felt the same about me.'

'You were not the only one who disliked him, Mr Morgan.'

'Sim,' he returned. 'It's what my friends call me.'

She was still. 'And am I that, then? A friend?'

'You are my wife, Adelia, and in private we can at least be polite to one another, can we not?'

He held out his hand and she gave him hers. It felt small in his grip and the ringless state made him frown.

'I think you lied about our engagement to save your family. At least I hope it was for that reason because anything else would be...'

'Dishonourable?'

She finished the sentence for him, but did not add further explanation.

'And I hope that you are not that.'

With care he let her hand go, watching as she withdrew it and folded her arms defensively.

'Life requires a certain ruthlessness to survive I have found, Mr Morgan. I have heard it said that you are ruthless in your sphere of work.'

He smiled. 'Perhaps my enemies might say that of me or men who failed in their quest to take a share in the fortune that the railways offer, but I hope I have always been fair.'

Her watching green eyes were bruised in uncertainty. 'Do you have family? There were none at the chapel.'

'I had an uncle.' He tried to keep the sadness from his tone, but her next query told him he'd been unsuccessful.

'And you wished that he might have been there? This uncle?'

Such perception worried him. If she could figure that out, what else might she come to know about him? There were so many damn things about his past that would shock her.

Leaning down to retrieve his necktie from the floor, he stepped away.

'I will send your missing jewellery back with my bookkeeper.'

'I am sorry.'

He paused. 'It is too late now, Adelia, for any regret.'

Once outside, he was glad for the air against his face and the sky above him. The last twenty-four hours had been mad, uncontrolled and frenzied. He could not remember ever feeling quite so uncertain.

A new bride. A wild ride north at night in a rented hackney. A shared bed and a marriage consummated to all intents and purposes.

Why had he come here? What had he expected might happen? It seemed any sense and logic he normally had were submerged by strong liquor. He had jumped from the frying pan straight into the fire and all by his own accord.

At least it seemed that this new wife might stick to those arrangements she had promised him at their very first meeting.

'I should not stop you from making your own personal choices. I would be compliant, dutiful and discreet. I would run the estate with diplomacy, refinement, grace and tact.'

Perhaps it could work. Perhaps in the machinations of controversy there lay a solution that was viable and possible. A marriage of convenience for them both, a formal and recognised contract that gave each of them their freedom. Not together, but apart.

He could stay in London and she could live here. He'd seen alliances with a lot less going for them in his lifetime and the few that were a love-match were often stormy with outbursts of desire, anger and fervour.

He couldn't expect love.

That thought came as easily as all the others.

No, this was the best he could hope for, perhaps, a woman who appeared much less prone to bad temper than the one he had imagined and a wife who might actually abide by the promises she had made him.

When the sun came out overhead he saw it as a sign and he was grateful when the old roan stallion in the Athelridge stable looked willing enough to ferry him into the nearby village.

Once back in London, Simeon spent the next few hours in the company of his bookkeeper, instructing him on his needs and wants.

Peter Shelman was curious about the news of the marriage and had questions.

'I haven't heard much mention of your new wife before, Mr Morgan. How did you meet?

'Her father and I knew each other.'

'Lionel Worthington? The Viscount? Wasn't he recently involved in some sort of carriage accident that killed his mistress? There were rumours that it was deliberate.'

Simeon decided he needed to be more honest. 'Worthington and I weren't actually friends.'

'I see.' There was a glint of puzzlement in the other man's eyes. 'I've heard talk of the daughter, of course, through my own wife's family. She is a rare beauty by all accounts.'

Everything Shelman was not saying was there in his face.

'She's a lot more than that,' Simeon returned. If his mother had taught him anything in life, it was the ability to fold the truth around a lie and make it stick.

Standing, Simeon found two glasses and a bottle. Better to pretend he was a happily married man or the difficult questions would start.

When he gave Peter Shelman a glass, his bookkeeper raised it high. 'Well, here's to marriage, then, Mr Morgan, and to your future.' Simeon was glad for the change of tone.

'So you wish for me to travel personally to Athelridge Hall and go over the accounts with Mrs Morgan? Are there limits to be placed on expenditures?'

'No. I want the estate running smoothly. Give my wife what she asks for and take someone with you who can identify the needs of an old building. I don't want it falling down around the family's ears.'

'You won't be there?'

'I won't.' He did not qualify that with more even as his bookkeeper turned his glass, the sunlight from a nearby window catching the crystal.

'I shall get back to you with the numbers, then, after I visit Athelridge Hall. I shall venture up there before the end of the week.'

'I look forward to your findings.'

Packing up his ledgers a few moments later, Shelman left, the lack of sleep and the effect of heavy liquor making Simeon feel tired, the bright light hurting his eyes. He did not know what Adelia might be to him. Lover? Enemy? Trickster? Helpmate? At the moment she was simply there, at Athelridge Hall, his wife of a day. Unknown.

The memory of the night they'd met at his town house was as strong as ever in his mind. Lust and desire held chains, he supposed, but they would never be enough. His first marriage and numerous subsequent mistresses had taught him that. He hoped she would not be too greedy in her demands for the estate and momentarily wondered if he should have placed a cap on her expenditures, but even that held the promise of difficulties he did not wish for.

If he had to have a wife in the wings, he wanted her content, for his childhood had shown him many examples of the vengeance of disgruntled spouses and it was never an easy thing to manage. No, reprisals and retribution were messy emotions that often led to even more misery; a misery he'd spent all the years since his childhood trying to limit.

He'd deliberately formulated a world of temperance and self-discipline around him until he had met Miss Adelia Worthington. Now all he could foresee was chaos and he wanted such confusion tempered and toned down wherever possible.

He was not a young green lad, for God's sake, but a twenty-seven-year-old businessman who had acquired a fortune in a game he could play with growing surety. He was usually even-tempered and unflappable, any emotion pared down to the barest minimum.

That was what had surprised him so much across all his dealings with Adelia Worthington and shamed him, too, though she was every bit as much to blame for the turn of affairs as he was.

Stop. Another voice sliced across his growing wrath. This bitterness was exactly what he did not wish to foster in himself. He would see to her needs and keep her happy and stay well away until he could truly decide just how to deal with her.

Their marriage of inconvenience.

He smiled at the thought and finished off the rest of his drink, the warmth of the brew softening his anger.

The bookkeeper Simeon Morgan had mentioned arrived at Athelridge Hall on the Wednesday of the week after their marriage.

He was tall and dour and as she led him into her father's office, Adelia felt as if she were being judged and found wanting. For the first time she saw Athelridge Hall through the eyes of another. Weary. Broken down. Worn out by a lack of money and of care. The man he had brought along with him was one who placed values on buildings and for a moment Adelia thought her husband meant to sell her home off to another.

'Your husband has asked that repairs of the larger structural problems be noted and duly begun, Mrs Morgan. My colleague is here to identify the problems. Is it all right if he has a look around the place?'

'Of course.'

She watched the man saunter off, his hands on the wall to his left as though even in feeling the stone he might understand the deficiencies in the place.

Taking Mr Shelman into the library, she gestured to the large walnut desk at one end of the room, watching as he removed a stack of notepaper and a small book from his brief-case. Sitting in the chair behind the desk, he laid out a pot of ink and a blotter, lifting his pen and turning it this way and that before writing Athelridge Hall in capitals on the first blank page and underlining it. Twice.

'I am here because your husband has instructed me to compile a list of things which need attention on your estate, Mrs Morgan. I presume from my brief look at the property on my way in here that the list of problems with the substructure will be a substantial one, so shall we begin with the things pertaining to the everyday running of the estate? I would like to hear about the expenditure that you feel to be the most important.'

Adelia swallowed. Goodness, what should

she say? How much did expenditure actually mean? Did this man have any idea of the true nature of her marriage and what was expected?

'My sister's health is not good. I would like to have enough ready money to be able to summon a doctor when I need to and to pay for any medicines required.'

Mr Shelman sat back without writing.

'Such expenses would best be taken from the weekly budget which you will be provided with.' He then mentioned a figure that was so generous she lost all her words. A weekly budget? A sum that would be repeatedly doled out week after week? Without end?

'Food. Heating. Servants' wages. Clothing. Furniture. Schooling. Transport. Medical bills. Miscellaneous. These costs are to be deducted from the weekly stipend, though if you have any need for more you would just have to ask and it shall be provided.'

'And my husband is aware of this sum?'

'He is. You would, of course, need to itemise all expenditure just to keep things above board, so to speak.'

'Above board?'

'Generosity can be taken advantage of if things are too laxly administered.'

'A state of affairs you would not allow?'

'Indeed not. I have worked for your husband for nigh on five years now and he is not a man who is easy to make a fool of.'

Adelia coloured. So Mr Shelman had heard the rumours of their marriage and he had come here with a warning. Was that at the bequest of his master or was this purely his own interpretation of how he found her personally?

She sat taller and placed her hands in her lap, stopping herself from wringing her fingers together. She could not refuse this offer because, if she did, then her mother and sister would suffer as would every other person working at the Hall. But God, she wanted to. She wanted to stand up and ask him to leave, to take his papers and his pen and simply go. But her pride, it seemed, was for sale as she made herself listen when he continued to speak.

'You will need to purchase a blank-paged book to make a ledger and write all expenses within it, without fail. I shall come to Athelridge Hall on the last Friday of each month to check the sums. Then on receipt of all being in order you shall be given your next advance. Personally, I think it is a very generous stipend allowed by Mr Morgan.'

'It is.'

'Your husband has asked me to prioritise any necessary remedial work about the hall as well, which is the reason my colleague has accompanied me today. This expenditure is additional and on top of the weekly budget. I imagine he is thinking of things like leakages or subsidence or breakages that are impeding the normal functions of the estate. Security is another issue that might bear some looking into. I am certain Mr Morgan wants you and your family to be safe.'

She smiled as he did and imagined the exact opposite.

Mrs Cranston had arrived now with a pot of tea and two cups and saucers and a few slices of fruit cake that had been baked that very morning. Adelia hoped Mr Shelman might stop with his business for a moment while they ate and drank, but this did not seem to be the case at all.

Rather, he took a sip of the tea and a bite of the cake and carried on regardless.

'Your husband is a man of wealth and talent, Mrs Morgan, but he is also a man who takes careful account of his money. I know your father, the Viscount, did not do this, so…'

At that insult he tailed off and sipped again at the hot drink.

'I shall be most careful to make the effort and account for everything.'

'Then I am glad of it. Mr Morgan also mentioned the fact that your very elderly servants might be of the age where retirement is upon them. He allowed provision for the hiring of younger servants.'

Adelia had suddenly had enough. 'Is that a suggestion or an order, Mr Shelman? I should certainly like to know where I stand in the use of my own common sense as stepping on people's pride may bring about a new set of problems, which I am keen to avoid.'

Unexpectedly he smiled and then quickly covered his appreciation with a frown.

'I am sure you know your husband far better than I do, Mrs Morgan.' A statement that held an undercurrent of doubt. 'I am also certain that you would know not to look a gift horse in the mouth.'

'I am twenty years old, Mr Shelman, and have the care of my ageing mother and very young sister. If there is one thing I do know it is this: wise care keeps what is gained and I shall be attempting to do just that.'

'Both in marriage and in money?' he asked next, and she understood in that moment why her husband used the man as his bookkeeper. The tenuous grasp she held on both was obvious to him, but he was warning her in a way that might be construed as advice. Keep your head up and your costs down and you have a chance of making this work.

She sipped at her own tea and felt the thump of her heart inside her chest.

Everyone in London must know now of this most unusual marriage. People talked and lawyers were people. Servants talked, too, and those in the town house on her first meeting with Simeon Morgan would have had a lot to say. Their marriage had hardly been a happy occasion and even ministers of God must have their opinions and voice them. The ripple effect of her deceitfulness would grow and such gossip would be keenly repeated.

Mr Shelman here was only doing his job by placing the terms of business on the table in much the same way as Simeon Morgan had laid down the conditions of their marriage. Conjecture was one thing, though, for no one truly knew the whole story and as long as they could keep up the pretence that there was nothing particularly unusual about their marriage there was a strong protection in that.

As the bookkeeper and surveyor left she saw Alexander Thompson on top of his white horse coming down the drive.

'Would you walk with me, Adelia? It is a lovely day and I have something of interest to tell you.'

Adelia had seen Alexander a number of times since his ill-thought-out kiss and each time he had seemed more and more morose. Still, it was difficult to simply refuse his offer of friendship and so, finding her hat and a light cape, she joined him, peering into the sky to see if there was any promise of rain.

After a few moments of walking, when he remained unusually silent she stopped to look at him.

'What's wrong?'

'I am worried about you, Adelia. Worried about Mr Morgan and his habits.'

Her heart sank.

'Habits?'

'I have been finding out about him,' he continued, ignoring her frown. 'And all that I hear is concerning.'

'To whom, exactly?'

'To me. To you. He has continued relations with his mistress despite his marriage. He pays for her lodging and expenses.'

'How would you know this?'

'I went up to London and talked with a Mrs Theodora Wainwright. Your mother gave me her name and she was easy to find.'

'Well, Mama has no business to gossip and neither do you, Alexander. What on earth were you thinking?'

'I went because of you, Adelia. Did you realise that he has a child living with him that is his?'

The image of the girl she had seen that first night flashed up in her mind's eye.

'How do you know this?'

'I have spoken with the governess, for I saw the child and the woman, a Mrs Wade, in the park. She confirmed it. She was most verbal about Simeon Morgan's shortcomings.'

The world tilted a little around Adelia. Could the child have been from his first marriage, the one that he had told her of? Was the girl the daughter of the wife who had died?

'Why would you do that? Why would you creep around behind my back and ask all these questions?'

'Because I love you, Adelia. Because you should not have married Simeon Morgan. Because I know now what should have happened, what could still happen if you were brave enough.'

'And what is that?' His declarations of love were unwanted and out of place and she sniffed discreetly to see if he had been drinking, but could not determine any scent of it on his breath.

'We could run away to America. Easy fortunes are to be made there, I swear it, and we could live together happily.'

'No. I could not do that.'

Real anger flashed in his blue eyes. 'There is only so much regret I can bear, Adelia, and I am coming to the end of it. True love is rare and wonderful and we have that, you and I, we have always had that. You know that we do.'

She had never seen him cry, but he started to sob now, tears running down his cheeks. 'Morgan is a man from trade. He has made a fortune, but it does not change what is in his blood. He is base and rough and an outsider. He will never love you as you deserve.'

The sky above was blue and the wind had

lessened, but Adelia felt as though she stood in a cold storm of unexpected emotion.

She could never love Alexander. He was a weak man with no sense of the world, a man who would pull her down into the mire just because of who he was. He was brittle, too, a product of being told since birth that he could have everything in this world if he only wanted it enough.

She tried to smile.

'Alexander, we are each of us on different pathways in life, which hold no promise of ever crossing over. I am sorry, but you have to realise that I have married Simeon Morgan and it is a union I mean to stand by.'

He began to cry more even as she continued.

'You have to find your own future now and it can be a good one. There are places you will see and women you will meet and...'

One hand began wiping away the tears in a manner that was harsh.

'No. Without much in the way of funding I am stuck here. You know that.'

After this outburst he turned and strode back towards the Hall, leaving her there to watch him, a lonely man with no family and very little hope.

Perhaps she should give him some of her allowance? Perhaps if she altered her figures a little in her ledger she might be able to see that he was at least cared for. She owed him that. The horror of everything fell down upon her because she knew in her heart that Alexander Thompson was tainted somehow and there was a time when she had very nearly thrown in her lot with him.

Simeon Morgan's visage shimmered before her and she prayed to God that he might come here to Athelridge Hall and see her if only for a day.

Chapter Six

Adelia was so very careful with the allowance Mr Shelman had handed her, relegating a great deal of it to a tin that she hid at the back of her wardrobe and keeping the rest out for all the day-to-day needs of a large estate and her small family.

It was more than her father had allowed her mother in years.

It was unbelievable.

A part of her wondered if it was blood money, a stipend to keep her away from London and uncomplaining, but the much larger part of her heart could only see the generosity despite the unusual visit from her husband's bookkeeper. She made a point of keeping some out for Alexander and sent old Cranston over to the Thompson estate with a parcel.

Noting the sum down in her ledger, she

wrote *Labour around Athelridge* and next to that *Mr Thompson*. At least the money was accounted for and she had a record of it for her own sake.

She had not seen Simeon Morgan for almost a month now and there were no plans in place to alter such a fact. If her mother wondered, she certainly did not voice any opinion and her sister Charlotte was far more settled and healthy with better food and less stress.

The ring and her gold cross had been returned, a carriage rolling into Athelridge Hall a day after Simeon Morgan had left. The thin gold ring she had fastened on to his little finger before their wedding had also been returned in the same package. There had been no note attached as a servant had handed her the jewellery. She had fastened the cross around her neck as soon as the conveyance had left, her wedding ring dispatched into a decorated pottery bowl, allowing the bauble a safe home.

She could not lose it, but she would not wear it. It seemed like a talisman of defeat with spinsterhood stretching before her in an unbroken line of forfeiture. A circle of pain and lost promises. A token of guilt and contrition, as well. She'd tried to write her husband a letter of thanks, but since every draft sounded worse than the last one she had given the endeavour up completely. If she'd been braver, she might have simply hired a carriage and gone to London to thank him personally, but there was always the chance that such an action might anger him given her solemn promise of not interfering in his life.

So she had made her bed and now she must lie upon it.

The box he had given her the night of their wedding as a birthday gift sat beside the bowl. The earrings were an exact match to her ring with their rose gold and emeralds. She had tried them on many times in her room alone at night, liking the feel of the draped gold and the way the baubles sparkled in the candlelight. She had never had such finery and enjoyed this hidden ownership.

A knock at the door made her start and the newly employed younger maid, Anna Stephens, stood there.

'There is a visitor downstairs, Mrs Morgan. He has come from London.'

Adelia's heartbeat quickened. Was it her husband? She resisted the urge to go to the mirror before following the girl out. Thank goodness she was at least in a dress that was presentable and her hair, while plainly tied back with a ribbon, was tidy.

Disappointment blossomed when she saw a servant waiting hat in hand at the front door and bowing as she came near.

'My master bade me to deliver this into your hands, Mrs Morgan, and to wait for an answer.'

Taking the letter, she broke the seal, seeing her husband's name scrawled at the bottom of the missive.

Simeon Morgan asked if she might come to London to stay at his town house in Carlton House Terrace. She was so surprised by the request she almost dropped the sheet of paper.

Why? Why would he suddenly want her there after all these weeks of no communication whatsoever? The note enquired if she could be ready to leave on the Thursday, mentioning something of an engagement at Lord and Lady Grey's house in Mayfair.

She remembered the Greys from her time in London. They were a middle-aged couple whom she had occasionally spoken with on the edges of the balls.

Other problems rushed in. Would her few

gowns left from last year's Season fit into this one's social events? Would she have to endure the same censure that she had suffered at the end of her extended time there? Would Rodney Anstruther and his family be in attendance, looking down their noses at her?

She could do nothing, however, but agree to her husband's request and, crossing into the blue salon, she found pen and paper and quickly scrawled out her reply.

Four days to be ready. Four days to try to formulate exactly what it was that she might say and act and do and wear.

The memory of his kiss at her breast in his bedchamber surfaced once more then, small jolts of heat in her stomach building up to stronger ones. Returning the missive to the Morgan servant, she watched him depart.

Simeon held his wife's answer in his hands and smiled.

At least she would come. At least he would keep Lord Grey happy in his wishes for some social communion and if he did not fit in entirely, then he knew that his wife would.

This was the part of business that he hated, the part where a certain humble and obsequious demeanour was required. Men like Lord Grey only believed in the notion of greater social equality to a certain degree. It was fine to invest in the business deal of a wealthy newcomer who had not the public standing he was more used to, but quite another thing to socialise with him. His wife, however, was a different matter as she had the connections of both title and an ancient estate.

Simeon would not even have imagined attending this dinner a month ago. The thought both amused and angered him.

But he needed Lord Grey's funds for the new push into connecting railway lines, his own money heavily promised to other schemes. He was being drawn thin across all his different endeavours in a way he had sworn never to be, the opportunity of new lines coming fast. If he did not put his hand forward, there was a danger of his expansion being hindered and cut off and bravery in business had always been his special distinction. Not unwise, but bold. Not foolish, but always escalating, a player in a field of others who watched his next move and copied him.

He stood and walked to the mantel, picking off the invitation he had received a week ago, the crest of the Greys displayed with pride and purpose.

He could not refuse this invitation even though he wanted to. He had seldom walked into the hallowed halls of the old money, preferring instead to operate in his own sphere, but he had come to a point where this was no longer possible.

Hell.

He hated relying on another person. He hated allowing himself to be beholden to anyone. He mostly hated having to send a pleading note to his wife who he had not seen for nigh on five weeks.

A knock at the door had him turning, and Mrs Wade, the governess, stood there with Flora Rountree at her side.

In all his ruminations he had forgotten the woman had asked for this meeting today. He placed Adelia's note in a drawer and sat behind his desk. He had expected Mrs Wade and Flora to sit, too, but they didn't. Rather, the woman pulled Catherine's child into line beside her and began to speak.

'I have asked to see you because your ward is under the misguided illusion that she may be going home soon. She seems to feel that her lessons therefore are a waste of time and has given no true endeavour at all to their learnings. I should like you to clarify her situation, Mr Morgan, just so that she does realise the true state of her tender here.'

Simeon looked down and saw a child who might have been himself nineteen years ago. Frightened. Indignant. Uncertain. The black rings under the girl's eyes gave the impression of a lack of sleep, her thinness indicating poor nutrition and the sores on her bottom lip pointing to the sort of stress that he himself had once known well.

He'd hardly given her a glance since her arrival here and that had been a mistake. He'd made sure she had a governess and was well housed and clothed and fed, but that had been it.

'Are you happy here, Flora?'

He tried to make his voice as soft as he could, but still saw a flinch of terror run through her.

'Yes, sir.'

Her reply was flat.

'Yet you do not enjoy your lessons?'

'I do, sir. I try.'

'I see. Do you go out with her, Mrs Wade? To the park or to the river. Or into town, perhaps?'

'Not often, sir. I am the governess. I am here to expand her mind. Books and writing are the tools with which I can do that.'

Simeon looked down at his desk. He had always been good at reading people and cursed himself for not recognising before what he did so plainly now.

Mrs Wade was patently unsuitable as a governess for this child.

Looking up, he took a calming breath. 'Could you wait outside for a moment, please, Mrs Wade. I should like a private word with my ward.'

The woman looked as if she might refuse, though as he continued to stay silent she eventually did as he asked, a final look at her charge confirming everything he had been afraid of. When she was gone, he asked Flora to sit, watching as she did so in that precise and careful manner fear engendered in young children.

'Your mother asked me to look after you, Flora, in a letter that was found in her lodgings after her death. Do you understand that?'

A single nod came back in reply.

'Your mother had no other family, no wider set of relations apart from a sister from whom she was estranged and who already has too many children of her own to take you in, but I was her friend so your future lies here under my protection. There is no one else to care for you.'

A flicker of desolation dashed across the small frightened face.

'But there is one thing I can tell you. I shall not fail you. You shall always have a home here with me until you no longer require it. Do you understand that?'

'I am…not…clever,' she returned as though this trait was the most important thing in all of the world.

'I do not require you to be.'

He gave the words as he might once have wanted them said to him. Without embroidery. Without question. A fact that was indisputable.

'I am not pretty, either.'

This took him aback. Who had told her that? Her mother? His intuition pinned such a criticism on Catherine Rountree. She had been both attractive and vain, a girl three years older than he was in the backstreets of Manchester and running wild. They'd enjoyed a friendship, but nothing more. By the time he was old enough to be attracted to her he'd understood the fatal flaw of her beauty and had never actively sought such perfection again. Until he had been pressed into a marriage with the most beautiful woman of them all.

'Show me your hands, Flora.'

Surprised, the child held them out, her long fingers pale and thin.

'A wise man once told me that hands hold life and that if you allow them good work you will always have happiness. I believed him and what he said turned out to be true. Is there something you would like to work on or with that you have not yet had the chance to?'

She shook her head.

'Think about it, Flora, and when you know I hope you shall tell me.' He waited for a second before asking his next question.

'Would you like me to find you another governess?'

Hope flared in small dark eyes.

'A kinder one, perhaps?'

'Mrs Wade will be angry...' she said and stopped.

'But you would like her to leave?'

Her head nodded instantly, no thought involved.

A shock of fury kept him still. Had the woman hit her or even worse? He would find out and then make sure the woman never worked as a governess again. She wasn't fit to care for children.

He rang the bell and waited as his butler came in.

'Could you take Miss Flora to the kitchens and ask the cook to give her something to eat, Harris? On the way out could you also send in Mrs Wade?'

'Of course, sir.'

An hour and a half later he was at the door of Theodora Wainwright. He had not seen her since the day of his marriage.

When she invited him in he went, hat in hand, and was relieved when she did not cross over to him, but waited for exactly what she knew must have been coming.

After firing the governess and asking Mrs Wade to leave immediately, he was in no mind to simply allow all the loose ends in his life to dangle around him. He needed to begin again in the way he meant to go on and, as a married man, he knew having a mistress was not a situation he was comfortable with.

'You are here to say goodbye, aren't you?'

Theodora got the question in before he could even start to speak and then she continued.

'I knew it would come to this, of course, Simeon. I have been dreading it for weeks.'

'I came to tell you myself and to say thank you for your company. I also come bearing a gift.'

He handed her a purse and she grasped it, taking a quick look at what was inside.

'You were always generous and honourable. If you ever change your mind...'

'I won't.'

'I know.'

'I hope you will be happy, Theodora.'

'Like you are?'

He found the grace not to answer that, for lies at this moment were what neither of them needed.

'I might go abroad, Simeon. America and the city of New York is tempting. A different life, a new start?'

He understood her frame of mind because his own was the same.

'Could I also give you something just to say goodbye.'

He nodded, waiting as she rifled through a drawer to one side of her bed and bringing out a small red-velvet book.

'They are poems I wrote for you.'

He took the offering even as he wished he did not have to, for something so personal and intimate was the last thing that he desired. But then goodbyes were seldom without mess and this was only a little quandary.

'There is also something that I wish to tell you about your new wife, something that you might not have heard.'

His interest focused.

'Ask her about the Honourable Alexander Thompson and see what she has to say about him.'

'Who is he?'

'A neighbour of hers who lives just outside the village of Athelridge. A *close* friend, by all accounts.'

Simeon did not like the way she said 'close', but he knew the harm of gossip and so he never listened to it. In fact, her words made it easier for him to leave her.

'I wish you well, Theodora.'

Outside, he closed his eyes briefly and smelt the call of autumn on the wind. His favourite season.

He had divested himself of a mistress and

a governess all in the space of one day and to-morrow he would finally see his wife again.

A street caller's shout made him pause and he stopped to purchase a bloater, delighting in the memory of the taste. If you were lucky, the herring had roe in its belly cavity and so it was two for the price of one. He could not ever imagine his wife thinking such fare a delicious treat and frowned as he took the offering.

Adelia arrived at midday on Thursday in London, the close push of traffic on the busy Northern Road holding her up. She came alone because her mother was sick and Adelia had asked the new young maid to stay back and look after her. There was no one else who could have accompanied her—the Cranstons were too old and her sister was too young.

The Morgan carriage sent to Athelridge Hall to bring her south was both comfortable and spacious and the driver and footman had been polite and helpful. Smoothing down the cotton of her dark blue gown, she hoped it was not too far out of fashion, for it had been one of her older dresses that had been refitted and differently trimmed.

The town house the conveyance finally

stopped in front of was the one she had visited the first time she had met Simeon Morgan all those weeks ago. In daylight it looked far more imposing.

She would be the mistress of the servants working here and that, too, was intimidating. She hoped she might play her part well, though she could not quite fathom what her husband might want of her.

As the front door opened, a trail of stiff-looking servants spilled out and within a moment her luggage had been transported inside and an older woman who introduced herself as Mrs Hayward, the housekeeper, led her up the staircase. The same butler she had met before smiled at her as she passed and tipped his head.

'Welcome to London, Mrs Morgan. I hope you had a pleasant journey.'

Upstairs, her room was a much paler version of the one she had come to the last time.

'This chamber has the very best view over the street,' Mrs Hayward said in a brisk way as she opened up doors that led to a balcony, 'and this is the best season to see the trees that line it.'

'Thank you. It all looks lovely.'

'The master will be here later, but if you

wish to have someone show you around the house before he comes—'

Adelia interrupted her. 'No, but I would like a cup of tea and then I shall unpack.'

'Of course. You have no lady's maid with you?'

'Unfortunately, I do not. My mother sickened yesterday with a chest complaint and so I left my maid at Athelridge Hall to attend to her needs.'

'Then one shall be provided, if you could give me just a little time, ma'am. A pot of tea and something to eat will be brought up to you now.'

When she left, Adelia sat down on the bed. She had a headache and a few moments of peace and quiet were just what she needed to recover, though the nervous energy of coming here made her feel slightly unbalanced.

Mama had barely spoken to her since the wedding and every time she did it was to reiterate her disappointment about the lack of a supper and celebration. It was as if the fact that her daughter's bridegroom had not made an appearance in over a month did not rate in importance at all. Adelia frowned, for given her father's lack of interest in his family perhaps this was what her mother imagined all unions to be like.

Providers of heirs and keepers of the house. She felt suddenly as lonely as she ever had in her life, marooned here in the city without any true intent and with a husband who was barely tolerating her.

Three hours later she was in the dining room, finishing her evening meal, when the door opened and Simeon Morgan swept in.

Today he was dressed all in black and with his dark hair and golden eyes he looked as dangerous and huge as she had ever seen him.

'I hope my servants have attended to your needs.'

He didn't say her name or give a greeting, and the awkward distance between them was so palpable she could almost touch it.

'They were very helpful, thank you, Mr Morgan.'

At her formal use of his name there was a slight twitch to his lips.

'You are settled in a room?'

'I am. A very pretty one upstairs with a balcony.'

'Good.'

The silence lengthened.

She could hear the tick of a clock in the corner by the windows and outside came the call of a bird in a nearby tree. A wren, she thought, the long jumbled bubbling interrupted by abrupt churrs and scolds.

'It is a fortunate aspect to have a park so close to your house.'

He made no answer, and she gritted her teeth. Dear Lord, this was going so much worse than she had imagined it might have. The ring which she had not worn until today glinted on her finger, mocking her, and she folded her hands into the copious fabric of her skirt to hide it.

'Would you like a drink?'

When she nodded, he crossed to a long low cabinet on one side of the room. After pouring out a good measure of white wine, he brought it over, his own libation in his other hand.

'To us,' he said then, and she almost dropped her glass in surprise, the 'us' he spoke of so non-existent and problematic. Was he jesting? His countenance did not suggest that he was and so she sipped the drink quietly.

The full body of grapes assailed her senses

and she took another. It had been so long since she had sampled something as delicious.

'I asked you to come to London because there is a dinner here in town in two days, one that I have no way of avoiding. A society dinner, I suppose is the best way to describe it, and one full of important men who hold an interest in the advancement of the railways.'

'As you do?'

He took a further sip of his drink and explained. 'It has been challenging to get to the place in business that I am at now, but if luck and fate have something to do with my success, then hard work is the true backbone of it. I should not like to fail at the last fence, so to speak.'

'And this dinner is the last fence?'

He smiled at that and she thought he should do it more often.

'Lord Grey, the man who is hosting the party, is an entrepreneur with very old-fashioned views. He wants to invest with me, but he has a need to know exactly who my family is before he can do so.'

'Your family?'

'You.'

One word that had her reeling.

'I know we are strangers and I know we have had our differences, but I would hope my help financially at Athelridge Hall might count for something and that you would agree to accompany me as a supporter to this dinner.'

'I know of him, this Lord Grey. He is said to be a good man.'

'Which is heartening.'

'He is also not a fool.'

'Less encouraging, that.'

Unexpectedly, she began to laugh. What was he wanting her to do? As if he had read her mind, he answered the question.

'I need a wife who might display diplomacy, refinement, grace and tact.'

She recognised his words as her own. It is what she had promised him on her very first visit.

'A wife who might bridge the differences between myself and Lord Grey.'

It was the only time he had mentioned his unusual background and because of it she was more honest, too.

'I doubt my name has much to recommend it. In truth, my father was not well liked.'

'Yet the connections of privilege still hold

power, Adelia, and these connections are the lifeblood of great fortunes.'

She liked the way he pronounced her name, with a long 'A' before it so that is sounded both different and exotic. She also liked the way he did not hide his true motives from her.

'Will you help?'

Her reply was given with caution. 'There were some in society who by the end of my time here in London might have a case to complain about my family's lack of funds.'

'You speak of the rental on the town house you were in?' He didn't wait for any answer. 'I paid off the debt. There will be no further objections on that score.'

A great weight lifted from her shoulders even as a complete humiliation and shame replaced it. She should explain herself, she knew she should, but what could she say? Her father's debts were many. She had tried to pay off all those she could, but that one was simply beyond her means and so they had fled back to Athelridge Hall, her shame and mortification complete and the constant and continuing demands for remuneration worrying.

'I owe you a considerable obligation, then, Mr Morgan, and one which I would be happy to discharge at the dinner you speak of and in the manner you require.'

'Call me Simeon. Sim is even better. Do you have a dress to wear? One that is suitable for such an occasion. I only ask because Mrs Hayward intimated you had brought a very small case with you.'

'I am not entirely sure if what I have brought would be fitting…'

'Then a seamstress will come to the house tomorrow to see to your needs.'

His tone of speech did not encourage argument, but she gave it anyway. 'The Athelridge Hall accounts you have been so generous with will pay for the cost of procuring a dress.'

He did not reply for a moment. 'Can I ask you something, Adelia?'

He waited till she nodded.

'Did you kill your father?'

Shock ran through her like a bolt of lightning. 'Who said that I did?' She fought for her words in the light of all he had just told her.

'Tom Brady. He is an inspector with the London Constabulary. He was there at our wedding and he said there have been whispers recently that you might have been involved.'

'Papa killed himself.'

'He told me that, too.'

'Then you know everything you need to and so does the inspector.'

Her prickliness was back again and he saw how her heartbeat raced in her throat. One step forward and then two steps back. He cursed himself for asking such a blunt question and sought a topic that was less inflammatory.

'My housekeeper said you had not brought a maid with you to London and that she has asked one of the girls from the house to aid you until we can find someone more experienced.'

'The girl, Christine, is more than adequate to meet my needs for the small time I shall be here. She has professed a great interest in the art of hairdressing as well and has asked if she can practise a style on me tomorrow. I am sure she will be sufficient.'

Most women of his acquaintance would never have been happy with an inexperienced junior maid, yet Adelia seemed to have no qualms whatsoever.

'Who did your hair in London when you were here for the Season?'

'I did it myself generally. I kept to simple styles.'

'Was your father with you much?'

'No. He wasn't a family man. But I think you know what he was like, Mr Morgan, so that truth cannot come as a surprise to you.'

'Did your mother not mind his...dalliances?'

'She is a Scottish woman who much prefers the quiet of Athelridge Hall over anything else society can offer. I am sure you must have already formed some opinion about her character, as well.'

'She seemed fearful.'

'People without certainty in their lives often are.'

'Unlike you?'

'I have always found it is easier to be...more direct.'

He laughed at that. 'Your baldly given deceit about your father giving me Athelridge Hall as your dowry being a case in point?'

She blushed, but stood very still.

'That was wrong of me and I am sorry for it. Usually I do not resort to lying.'

'And your use of my drunkenness on the night of our wedding?'

'You came to me, Mr Morgan. When you fell over I had few options.'

'Apart from scrambling into bed behind me and pretending we had consummated our marriage?'

'Annulling our marriage because of non-consummation would be as damaging to your reputation as anything else might be. Better to have a wife far from London who would make no fuss at all about anything you should wish to do.'

'The carte blanche you promised me?'

'Exactly.'

'Did such a policy make your mother happy?'

'It did not, but then I am not my mother.'

'So your sole purpose of pressing for this marriage of ours was to keep your family content?'

'Put like that, I suppose you could say it was.'

'A sacrifice for the greater good?'

'And one to escape the obvious bad.'

'Like homelessness?'

'If you have never faced such a thing, you may not understand the difficulties inherent in such a state, Mr Morgan.'

'But I have, Adelia, and many a time, too.'

'When you were young? Society paints a picture of a childhood that was hardly easy.' She looked interested, her green eyes focused fully upon him.

'I found that the bottom of the barrel had its advantages for any small slice of luck or fortune can only lead one way. Up.'

'So you did not simply surrender to your fate?'

Simeon Morgan seemed taken aback by her question and, instead of answering, he turned to finish his drink, looking outside the window at the trees opposite bending in the breeze of an early autumn dusk.

She had never had such a conversation with anyone like this before, full of innuendo, secrets and some vague anger, but underplayed by a truth that was startling. He had allowed her to see into his life, into his difficulties, because she had done the same. Was this a pathway that would allow them some growth? As it stood they'd always been balanced on the opposite sides of the spectrum. His mistress. Her family. Her need. His bounty. Her place in society and his place out of it. Opposites in nearly every way she could imagine and yet...

With the lights shining on the darkness of his hair, she saw a hue of a deep and startling red, the darker tone of his skin alluding to ancestors from sunnier climes than that of a cold and pasty England. The jacket he wore stretched across his shoulders, outlining the muscles beneath. Not a sedentary man, she thought, and not a weak one. She remembered back to the first time they had met, the sheen on his bare chest and his trousers moulded around masculine flesh in a way that had sent colour to her cheeks then, as the mere memory of it did now.

He was not vain like those lords she had been introduced to in society, full of their own self-importance and their rather feminine beauty. No, Simeon Morgan would run circles around all the frail and delicate men of note with his menace, his fierce intelligence and his truths. She wanted to help him make his railway empire. She wanted the luck he hadn't been born with to continue and the fact that he had asked for her assistance made her feel powerful after so many years of vulnerability and hopelessness.

Although she might not expect love from this marriage, mutual respect lay in a good second place. Her own father had not respected her mother and look at the catastrophe there. For the first time in months a small worm of hope wriggled to the surface, an optimism that Adelia had not expected from such a betrothal, and the potential to at least be needed was a confidence that delighted her.

The wine was doing its work, too, softening worry and alleviating concerns.

'Society holds its own patterns of control over those who were not born into the ruling classes, Mr Morgan, but I always thought that such authority had its limits. People like you worry the aristocracy for they resent the equal status of an intelligent and rising merchant class. Instead, they wish for the old status quo and the continuation to rule unthreatened themselves, despite their many shortcomings.'

He frowned at that and gave her answer. 'Change can be productive for everyone should the aristocracy loosen their grasp on desperation and listen to what is being said.'

'Which is...?'

She was thrilled with the way he sought her opinions, giving his own back in the manner that his past had informed him. He was not condescending or patronising by any means for the traditional boundaries between classes were being eclipsed at a rapid rate and he knew it.

'Every man deserves a sense of social place that relies on respect.'

'It is my opinion Lord Grey would hold to that.'

'But there are many who refuse to.'

'Because they are scared?'

'Well, change is always confusing and it takes time to accept it.'

'But you don't have that? Time, I mean, for the building of your railway?'

He laughed then, loudly.

'With you at my side I might manage it.' He held up the bottle of wine in a silent offer of more, but she shook her head.

She needed all her wits around a man like this, a man who kept changing on her, one moment distant and the next congenial. One moment a product of his upbringing and the next a captain of industry who was nobody's servant. He spoke with wisdom and honesty and was not unsettled by the fact that she returned her advice in the exact same way. He did not stifle her or reprimand her. He did not bore her, either.

The clock in the corner struck the hour of nine, reminding them of the passing of time and the oncoming night. The real world crept back in, the problems and the reality of what they were to each other. Or weren't.

'You must be tired after your journey. I will bid you goodnight, Adelia. I hope my housekeeper has provided you with all that is needed.'

'She has.'

The awkwardness was back and the detachment. With a small tip of his head he was gone, disappeared into one of the many rooms of this vast house, vanished from her.

Her left hand lay on the table and her wedding ring caught the light.

Not yours, it said. *Be careful.*

Such changing whims of fortune sent her head spinning, the wine strong and potent.

'Just like Simeon Morgan himself,' she whispered and stood, a servant coming forward to help her from her chair. Tomorrow was another day and she would face it as it came. Tonight, although she was exhausted, she also felt alive and animated and the distant turmoil she was more accustomed to was a long way from here.

She walked back up the grand staircase and wondered who the portraits lining the walls were of, grand people rendered with an excellence in tempera and oils. Perhaps they had come with the house when he had purchased it and he had simply left them there, a replacement for all his missing family and the history he had never had.

'You. My family,' he had said, and she felt the warmth of this statement settle in around her heart.

She dreamed that night of her father.

The gun was pointed at her, the dark stare of death and his finger on the trigger. She smelt the alcohol on his breath and saw the scratches she had left across his cheek, deep and weeping, from defending herself as he had lashed out at her with his fists.

'You've never been easy ever since you were a child with your set opinions and your arrogance and all the beatings I gave you made no damn difference.'

'Respect was all I have ever asked for from you because I understood that there could never be more.' She resisted adding the word

Papa. It had been so long since she had called him that.

She felt the bruises where he had hit out at her intransigence, felt the wounds inside, too, from a lifetime of living with a man who'd always hated her. She stood there, daring him to pull the trigger, strong with fury and bitterness and hurt. She did not look away. For so many times and over so many years her father had been a violent and brutal man, punishing her with his fists and his anger, making her understand that he was to be obeyed in everything and at all times. There was no sense in him, no wisdom, no fairness that she might have understood. It seemed every word or expression he did not like was another reason to discipline her.

But the use of a firearm to threaten her was a new thing. 'I hope the husband you finally manage to procure will force some sense into your stupid head, though God knows who would ever want you with your ridiculously high standards of behaviour. It's why your Season was such a failure and all the damned money I spent on that rigmarole went to nothing. They could see it, those young men, see the rot inside you...'

She laughed at that because diffidence was the only weapon that might dissipate his anger and because suddenly she simply did not care.

If he killed her, then that was that, but if he didn't she could not see how they might go on from here.

'Your mother at least learnt what her place in the world was. You, on the other hand, have opposed me every single moment you could, you have questioned my authority as the head of the house and thrown it back in my face. You are a lying bitch with all your criticisms of me and I am sick to death of your righteous and holier-than-thou ways.'

'Just as I am sick of you, Lionel, and I wish to God that you were not my father.'

As his grip and the direction of the gun altered she drew in a breath and when the gun went off all she saw was empty space where his face had been one second before. Her words had killed him, Adelia thought then, and a guilt unlike any other had risen inside her. She had finally told him exactly what she had thought of him and this was the result.

A hand pulled her back into the night, into the room, into the now, and her husband was leaning across her, dark and frowning.

'You were shouting out. I thought...'

He stopped, and she scrambled up, ruching the sheets, rearranging her shift, panting in fright. She couldn't stop shaking, her breath coming in gasps and the light spots obscuring her vision as they always did after a nightmare. He had her head down in her lap before she could stop him, his fingers threading through her unbound hair, the sweat on her scalp a damp coldness.

'Just breathe slowly, don't hurry it.'

She did as he said, her thready heartbeat slowing, the dizziness diminishing and the images of death fading. Shame flooded into the spaces where fright had lingered, leaving only humiliation. Shaking him off, she tried to find her inner reserves of strength.

'I am sorry for waking you.'

'You didn't. I was reading.'

Her eyes went to the clock. Two thirty. Outside, the darkness was bathed in silence. Even the wind was quiet. She watched as he pulled a chair out from the small writing armoire and sat down on it, his long legs stretched in front of him. The collar of his shirt was loosened and he wore neither necktie nor waistcoat.

'Do you often have bad dreams?'

This was asked simply.

'Sometimes.' She did not wish to tell him that she always felt so scared she could barely take in air. She did not say that for so many years she had not slept properly just in case...

'You called out for me to help you. You used my name.'

A flush of horror stained her cheeks.

'You also cried out to your father to stop.'

This was a more complex statement and deserved an answer.

'I was there when he shot himself and there was blood. Everywhere.'

'That was the same day I met you for the first time, yet you didn't behave like a woman who had just seen her father blow his brains out.'

'Because I was glad when he did it. I thought he meant to take me with him, you see, and all I could feel was utter relief and then guilt.' The truth flooded from her, unstoppable.

'Dear God.'

She almost smiled at his blasphemy, but didn't. He could not want to be landed with all these problems, a woman who had tricked him into marriage and now was turning into someone with a growing set of personal disasters behind her. She remembered the beautiful woman whom he had brought to their wedding. Perhaps she was someone he had a great love for. Alexander had certainly intimated it to be so. Perhaps her own insistence on a union between them had ruined Simeon Morgan's life in a lot more ways than she had thought of. Was she still ruining it? She was hardly a prize and yet here he was in the middle of the night, trying to comfort her.

With care she began to speak because it might be her only chance to say this. 'There are so many things that we each of us do not know about the other, Mr Morgan, but perhaps there could be civility at least in our relations? Enough civility to make our situation liveable?' She tried to imbue a lighter note into her words so that he might agree and was pleased to see him nod his head.

'Problems always seem worse at night, Adelia. Remember that. Will you be able to sleep now?' The question was softly asked.

'Yes. Thank you.' She bit down on her lower lip in the attempt at a smile. More lies.

He stood then and walked to the door, but once there turned and waited as if he was trying to formulate exactly what he might say.

'I do not allow my past to define me and I did not have an easy childhood. I would suggest you try to do exactly the same.'

When he was gone she thought about his advice and what it meant for her. For so long she had been scared to live. For so many years her sole purpose had been the protection of her family. Finding food, providing wood for warmth, believing that it would get better if only they waited long enough.

Civility.

She rolled the word on her tongue and felt the lack in it. Simeon Morgan had allowed Athelridge Hall a generous stipend. She liked talking to him. She enjoyed the way he looked at the world. His honesty surprised her.

Her fingers stroked across the sheets and stilled. If she was truthful she wanted a lot more than simply conversation. She wanted what he had shown her that first time when his tongue had skimmed across her nipple and made her feel things she never had before.

Civility.

Such a formal and stiff word.

Almost on a par with pity.

Chapter Seven

Simeon strode back to his room and sat looking out of his window. He felt keyed up and furious, all the things that his wife had told him weighing on his mind.

Perhaps it explained who she was and what she was. Hard-hearted. Cold. Single-minded. Deceitful. She'd had to be all those things simply to survive. She'd probably had no one to stand in her corner in the draughty halls of Athelridge Hall. Certainly her mother would have been no help at all and her sister was too young.

She'd arrived here in London alone, without even a maid. That should tell him something. Her bag had been small and she had eaten the offered evening meal with the sort of relish that echoed of true hunger. Other thoughts gelled.

What sort of a life had she truly lived? Where were all the gowns he had imagined she had accumulated from her last spectacular Season? She had known she would be going to a dinner party when she had come here, so why had she not thought to bring suitable attire?

The gowns were gone. That thought came next. Given that she hadn't had the money to pay for the London accommodation for her Season, the clothing would have brought in something to tide her family over until she'd married him.

Her Season had been a failure so he could only imagine how her father might have reacted to that. Lionel Worthington was a man who would have been quick to give his opinion and Catherine Rountree had implied he was handy with his fists.

He remembered the bruises on Adelia when she had come to him that first time, fresh bruises applied with force. She'd said she'd thought her father might blow her brains out and could imagine her fright and relief when he didn't. She'd come to see him the same night because to wait any more might have negated the purpose, her father's death untimely and inopportune.

Tom Brady had said the family had kept it quiet for a few days and he could well see why. She'd needed time to find a husband who would see them safe and because he had the papers to Athelridge Hall he was the first and obvious choice. Suicide was against the law of God and, once the title went and the Worthington finances were uncovered, she knew there would be little hope in snagging any lord of the realm.

The safety of her family, the retention of her home and the buffer of a man who was wealthy to boot. No wonder she had come to see him and had not been frightened off when he'd told her to undress.

Desperation held depth. Of all the people in the world who might know that, it was him. She'd lied and she had kept on lying.

The clock in the corner chimed three thirty and there was a lightening in the eastern sky.

Theodora's gossip about the man named Alexander Thompson also came to mind. Had Adelia lied about her virginity and her innocence, as well? Somehow he suspected that she must have for Peter Shelman had visited him today with the ledgers and he'd seen Alexander Thompson's name listed alongside a sum of money provided for non-specific *services*.

The awkwardness of all these truths was wearying and he had no idea what would happen if he confronted her about them. Innocence was a ploy many a young girl had used to their advantage and who was he to judge her for relationships he himself had enjoyed for years? It was the lying he abhorred.

He shook his head and tried to think.

God, the dinner party looked less and less appealing, yet he was committed to attend.

He would contact the dressmaker in the morning at least and pay the woman well for her immediate services. With an appropriate gown Adelia might be less likely to try to get out of her promise to help him, though he wished again that he had not accepted the invitation in the first place for civility had the sound of severity to it.

What exactly did it mean?

He had not seen her for over a month since the wedding. He had not bedded a woman in all that time either and he was coming to the conclusion that he was a man who needed to feel intimacy again. Teddy was off limits because of his marriage and he could not find it

in himself to visit one of the high-class pros-
titutes that catered to private and anonymous
needs such as his own.

His marriage began to have a bite to it that
he had not expected, the sting of celibacy a
barb that dug into his skin and made him irri-
table. Tonight as his wife had been drawn from
sleep, her soft curves on show, feelings had
awoken in him that he had tried hard to ignore.

This marriage kept changing on him, that
was the problem. The certitude he'd felt on
going into such a sham had diminished as he'd
understood his lack of options. His childhood
had been full of men who were fickle and unpredictable, his mother's poor decisions adding to the problem. He'd promised himself that
disloyalty in the marriage bed would never be
his lot and stuck to widows or courtesans instead. Until Adelia had rushed headlong into
his life with her deceits and promises and he
had washed up on the impossible foreign shore
of no choice.

He wished he could go back and handle this
another way, but he had been caught in her
bed by his own mistake and now there was no
route of escape.

Civility. For all the many years of his life.

Civility stretching into for ever. Simeon had the sudden thought that Lionel Worthington must be laughing at him all the way from his place in hell.

Finishing the rest of his drink, he looked at the clock. An hour till he could get dressed and leave the house. He'd go and see Tom Brady for an early breakfast and then he would send a note to the dressmaker.

He was not a man who had ever waited for life to happen to him. His uncle had put it succinctly when he had told him again and again that the habit of waiting was unproductive. He smiled, imagining Jamie seeing him here, so ambiguous, so undecided. No, after this dinner party, things would move on from where they stood now between himself and his very new wife. He would make certain of it.

Adelia was dressed in the most beautiful gown she had ever worn. The silk of the coffee-coloured dress swirled around her, the low neckline and elongated bodice showing off her figure as nothing else had. The sleeves were tight at the top, but expanded at the elbow to fall in a funnel shape to her wrists. She wore a horsehair crinoline for shape, extra layers of flounces and petticoats further emphasising the fullness of her skirts and narrowness of waist.

The late morning and early afternoon had been spent in the company of the dressmaker, Madame Sylvie Ferrier, as she had run through her stock of ready-made gowns and finally settled upon this one. Another few hours of pinning, fitting and primping had produced the result Adelia now saw and she couldn't remember a gown that moulded to her body so well or felt so comfortable.

Christine had braided her hair into three plaits and tucked them up in a style that was complicated. Two silk roses in pale cream sat in the roll of hair on her left side. Long white gloves and silken slippers completed her outfit.

Looking in the mirror in her chamber with her maid beaming behind her, Adelia barely recognised herself.

'It is not too low?' Her fingers fussed with the bodice, trying to pull it up a little.

'You will upset the line of the ruching if you do that, madam.' Christine stepped forward and tugged it down again. 'See. It is made to be exactly this way.'

Today she was wearing the emerald earrings

Simeon Morgan had given her on the night of their wedding. Her hair shone pale in the light, small tendrils of wayward curls escaping round her face and softening the effect of the thick braids.

Christine had also applied some make-up, something Adelia was initially shocked by, but the end result was highly flattering and very understated. Her eyelashes looked darker with the kohl and her cheeks were pink from the moistened red-tissue paper that had been dabbed on sparingly.

'All the women wear it, madam, even though they say they don't. I like to keep up with these things, you see, because one day I shall be a proper lady's maid and won't have to work at all the tasks downstairs.'

'Well, you have done a wonderful job, Christine, and I thank you for it.'

The small maid smiled. 'You would look beautiful in a sack, Mrs Morgan, and that is not something I could say about anyone else.'

For so long now Adelia had received compliments about the way she looked so that they were almost a routine part of meeting new people. The only one who had never truly complimented her was her husband. Her thoughts then went to the red-headed woman at their wedding. Perhaps he preferred a more overt beauty, more voluptuous and worldly.

Dabbing some rose-scented cream on her wrists and her neckline, she took a steadying breath and began to walk to the stairwell.

Simeon looked at the clock and finished his brandy. His wife would be down soon, he was sure of it, his housekeeper's assessment of how wonderful she looked highly reassuring.

He hoped that tonight would go well. He hoped that they would seem sufficiently like a happy couple to pull the charade off. He needed Lord Grey's capital to complete this portion of railway line for without it the whole stack of his other investments could fall into pieces leaving him with a gaping hole in his resources.

He seldom gambled on anything that he had and he did not like the feeling one little bit. Swearing beneath his breath, he placed his empty glass down on the mantel just as Adelia came into the room.

She looked completely different from how he had ever seen her before. She looked regal and majestic and noble, a daughter of high society elegantly on show from the top of her coiffured flower-strewn hair to the heels of her bejewelled satin slippers. She looked untouchable.

He felt like a six-year-old again, sent by his mother to the back doors of the fancy houses to deliver the face creams she had begun to make.

Not belonging. Out of his depth.

'The colour suits you.' His hand waved in the general direction of the gown even as he tried to determine what the name of such a hue was. Neither brown nor cream, it sat halfway, the material catching the light and moving in a manner that was fascinating.

'Thank you.'

Her smile was secretive and her cheeks glowed pink.

'Would you like a drink before we leave? There is still some time before the carriage will be brought around.'

When she nodded he poured her a brandy, refilling his own glass in the process and holding it up.

'To tonight.'

A fleeting humour filled her eyes, but then some other emotion crossed her face.

'I have to warn you that I did leave society under a cloud after my Season.'

'But you have the umbrella of my money now and wealth speaks with an eloquence duly noted here in London.'

'A lucky thing, that.'

He was unsure whether the words were exactly as she said them and he swallowed, trying to find his balance. Adelia had knocked him sideways this evening with her beauty, like a butterfly hatched from its cocoon and knowing full well how it now appeared.

She was his wife in name only, though she had once offered to be a lot more. That thought both aroused and annoyed him at one and the same time and this made him frown further. In all truth the promise between them was shaky and false and, looking as she did now, he knew that she was bound to attract the attention of every eligible man in the room. He chased that thought away and concentrated on what he did have. At least she was wearing the earrings. The emeralds matched her eyes, her eyelashes dark against the paleness of her skin.

The bodice was low. He could see the rise of her breasts easily above it. Would she wear a shawl to cover the flesh? Should he say something about the display? Should she be more covered, with less on show?

For heaven's sake. He was becoming the sort of man he had always hated. Irresolute. Undecided. Insecure.

He set his jaw.

'Lord Grey will want to know what you think of me. If you concentrate on the words responsible, trustworthy and sensible, that should be enough.'

Her raised eyebrow worried him.

'Do you think I am those things, too, Mr Morgan?'

He could not understand her drift as he answered, 'I do not know you well enough to say.' He realised the moment he had spoken that this was exactly what she was after.

'Touché,' he added quietly and smiled.

'It might be good if you tell me a little about your hopes for the railway line you wish Lord Grey's help with.'

She said this simply, with no sarcasm in it, so he formed an appropriate reply. 'It's a northern route and the roads in the west are in poor condition at the moment and make slow travelling for goods or passengers needing to be transported between Birmingham and London.

The speed that trains travel despite any sort of weather means healthy perishables can be delivered more cheaply and reliably, something that can only benefit those with smaller resources who are largely unable to access such products now.'

'You are a socialist then, Mr Morgan? A man who would have wealth shared around?'

'I'd say I am more of a realist and it's not all altruistic. Unless this part of the route goes ahead a lot of the other lines that I have had a hand in putting into place will fail to prosper.'

'And who would the rights to lay down more railway lines revert to if you cannot deliver?'

'Those who have held the ancient privileges will undoubtedly say it is in their domain. But I believe that progress now lies in the hands of men who would dream of what is to come, men who know the other side of luck and would strive for the betterment of everybody.'

'Merchants like you?'

The question came back quickly and he frowned. 'To be a merchant is not quite as base as you might think it. Men with vision can now claim a part in the future with as much certainty as those who have ruled in the past.'

She did not answer his declaration. Instead, she asked another question entirely.

'Where did you learn about all this, Mr Morgan? What learning formed your thoughts?'

'My great-uncle was the instigator and he saw to my education in various engineering workshops around Manchester. After that I opened my own firm where I quickly learned everything else that I needed to know.'

'A man of wide experience, then. That should please Lord Grey.'

'I imagine he knows all these things about me already, Adelia. No one invests great amounts of money without checking on the past of the one they are entrusting with their hard-earned fortune and that period of my life is easy to verify.'

'Oh, I doubt Lord Grey's fortune was hard earned. It is said his grandfather left him everything after his father disappointed the family.'

'I didn't know that.'

'Did you know that his wife is from Scotland and that her great-grandfather was one of the powerful Northern Barons? Many say he was an evil man, a man who threw tenants off his land with an alarming carelessness and thought nothing of it.'

He shook his head.

'Which in itself goes to show that very few in society have a past that is lily-white, Mr Morgan. Dig deep enough and there are hidden skeletons in every affluent aristocratic closet.'

'Including yours?' The two words held more gravity than he intended and she turned at that and finished her brandy.

'No one is perfect and if your motives for this railway are as honourable as you state them to be, then that is all the armour you will need.'

The thought of being in society left him cold. The only reason any one of these lords had given him purchase was because they knew he could make great sums of money for them. He was seldom invited into the inner sanctum of their private social occasions.

Tonight was different and he knew that it was only because of Adelia that the invitation had been sent to him in the first place. He wondered again how the night might go and what sort of impression they would leave.

'Grey is expecting a newly married couple. If you could find it in yourself to remember that...'

'And pretend?' she shot back.

'I imagine that you would be very good at that.'

'Perhaps you are right.' Her voice was quiet.

When the butler knocked at the door a moment later announcing that the carriage was ready, Simeon straightened his shoulders, waiting patiently as she donned a light cloak, and then followed her out into the night.

The three rooms on the first floor were large, opening out on to each other with sets of double doors and the walls were covered in elaborate papers, Old Master paintings and gilded mirrors, every surface holding porcelain, silver and glass.

The middle dining room was appointed with large tables, buffets and sideboards, the placements set out '*à la Française*' style, in which the food, when it came, would allow the host and hostess to display their wealth and prestige through the sheer size and splendour of the table.

She had never been to a town house of such magnificence before and she could well see why it was said to be one of the most elegant examples in the whole of London. She was also aware of the sidelong glances given her from the others present, a woman who was not quite welcome here because of the various rumours that had swirled about her early exit from the London Season and the instability of her family.

Simeon, however, looked relaxed beside her, his large stature in a room of small men making her smile. He did not appear to be the least bit overawed or uncomfortable, which made her wonder anew at his need to have her here.

There were many more guests present than she had thought there would be and she recognised some of them. One of the woman, Mrs Mavis Trenwith, came straight across to her, her eyes wide with supposition. Adelia remembered her as being a close friend of Mr Rodney Anstruther, the suitor who had tried to kiss her in the park. Simeon was speaking with a man she did not know to his left and so Mrs Trenwith held her full attention.

'I heard you had snared a fortune in marriage, but barely believed it, Mrs Morgan, for we have not seen you back in London at all, especially after your hasty last exit.'

'I have been busy organising Athelridge Hall and Mama has been unwell.' She remembered the woman's meanness when she had been here last time with an ache of worry, though as if on cue Simeon turned, his smile taking in the woman in a way that made Mrs Trenwith blush vividly.

'We decided we should probably spend some time in the city, didn't we, Lia?' He took her hand and tucked it into the crook of his arm. His nickname for her was new, as was the way he glanced across at her, his intensity giving the impression of a groom more than proud of his new bride.

'I did not hear much about your wedding.' Mrs Trenwith stated this, though with much less confidence than she had appeared to have a moment ago.

'It was a small one and then afterwards we were too busy celebrating the nuptials to worry about others.' Simeon's explanation was returned with warmth.

'A fortuitous alliance, then?' An undertone of criticism was evident.

Adelia knew that she should be adding something to Simeon's efforts of make-believe and so she joined in.

'Indeed it was, Mrs Trenwith, and because of it we shall be forever blessed.' Her grip tightened on her husband's arm as Lord Grey came forward and she was relieved when Mavis Trenwith moved away.

'You don't like her?' This was said quietly, though, and as Adelia shook her head he turned to acknowledge their host.

'Lord Grey.'

'It's good to see you here, Mr Morgan, and I am so glad you could both come. My wife is most eager to speak to you of your wedding and here she is now, scurrying over. Mr Morgan, you must come and meet my brother and his business partner as they have asked me for an introduction. Would you allow me a moment with your husband, Mrs Morgan?'

'Of course.'

But she did not take her hand from Simeon's arm easily, the sense of safety she felt here next to him diminishing rapidly as he went.

Lady Grey was all quiet attention and kindness. 'Oh, my dear, I am most interested in hearing every last detail about your wedding. I said to my husband that Mr Morgan deserved a singular wife to stand by his side and I know he will have found it in you—'

But she broke off that train of thought and began on another.

'Tell me how you met your elusive groom, for Mr Morgan so seldom graces any of the society events.'

'He had business with my father.'

'I had heard that. Your mother must have been pleased to be able to stay at Athelridge Hall, though, for I know she always loved the place and she would have been utterly devastated to lose it.'

Adelia had forgotten that Lord Grey's wife had known her mother once.

'When my husband informed me of your match I thought it was the perfect union. Your time here in society had its difficulties, I know it did, but a man who can stand up to any pressure exerted is exactly the one you want and Mr Morgan by all accounts is well able to do that. There is a certain power inherent in his unusual background, I suppose, and society must amuse him no end.'

Adelia used this opening to press forward her husband's case.

'I know he highly values the business he does with Lord Grey. He had told me a little of the rail tracks that he has had a hand in putting down and his dreams for a line that might open up the north to the advantage of all.'

'He speaks to you, then, of his business?'

The question was framed in a way that made Adelia hesitate, but then she decided to be honest.

'He does. I like to think there is a great deal of trust between us.'

'As there is in my own marriage, my dear.' Lady Grey reached across and took her by the arm.

'Come and meet my sister, for I am sure you will like her and she you.'

Within minutes Adelia was ensconced in a group of close Grey family relatives and enjoying the company, this sort of a gathering so much easier than those she had been subjected to during her Season in society earlier on in the year.

After ten or so minutes, Simeon came back to rejoin her with Lord Grey in his wake. He moved straight to her side and she felt him there, large and looming, his presence allowing her the sort of feeling of well-being she was astonished by. She wished he might reach out for her hand again, but he did not, merely standing and chatting with an older man next to him while sipping at a drink he held.

All over the room women watched him.

That thought made her swallow. During her Season men had observed her like that, but here another set of values was in play.

It was not beauty that drew them to him, but power. In the company of all those here she could well see what she had missed when they had been alone. Simeon was beautiful in the manner of a man who had seen life and moulded it exactly to his wishes, a man who had come through a baptism of fire to arrive at the place he was always meant to be. A leader and a visionary. The thought that they all wished for the shine of his success to rub off on to them even for a little while came to her next.

The very truth of it made her feel incredibly guilty. She had tricked him into this marriage for her own purposes, never giving a thought as to his true vocation. She felt shallow and one-dimensional, a woman who had thought only of her family's needs and completely omitted his. A woman who had imagined beauty to be the only currency men traded in and had disregarded other pathways offering far greater value.

Her husband could have petitioned any

woman in society to be his wife and they would have jumped at the chance. No wonder he had refused her offer with such conviction.

She had come here tonight, expecting to be a guiding light in all matters pertaining to navigating society, and found out instead that he could do that without hesitation himself. He was a chameleon who adapted without difficulty into any new environment.

'You look pensive.'

His words whispered close brought her from her thoughts.

'I think even you must realise how little you need me here to smooth your way, Mr Morgan,' she murmured back.

'But it helps,' he returned and took her hand in his, kissing the back of it quietly. Shock roared through her until she looked up and saw Lady Grey watching them closely.

An act, the sham of it mortifying because for a moment she'd imagined that he might have meant the intimate gesture, that perhaps his feelings for her had changed and he wanted a new start, a closer understanding. With as much aplomb as she could muster her fingers tightened around his.

'Every woman in the room gives the impression that they want you and I doubt it is just your money they are after, either.'

He began to smile. 'What else could it be, then?'

'Power holds a certain aphrodisiac and when it is packaged in a man who seems to give no care for all the absurdities of grand society—'

He interrupted her.

'You think I don't?'

'I think you laugh at us even as you weave your schemes with such dexterity around the archaic notion of inherited wealth and privilege.'

'I disagree. There is always some essential danger in stepping over lines.'

This time it was she who laughed. 'If there is, Mr Morgan, I can assure you that you hide your worry well.'

'Perhaps you are the mirror I need, then.' His lips came down across her hand again, and she felt his warmth with an ache.

'Stop it.' She almost growled the words, her pasted smile there only for the sake of appearance.

'You said you would help. You promised me grace,' he countered wickedly.

'We can act married without the pathos of such deceit.'

'What books do you read to speak this way? You do not sound like any other young lady I have ever met.'

She felt the blush crawling up her cheeks. Reading had been her one way of escaping her life and she had devoured every book in Alexander's extensive library. It was why her Season had finished the way it did, she supposed, because finally she could no longer pretend to talk about small nothings.

'The library at my town house is a substantial one, Adelia. I would be interested to see what you think of it.'

'You read a lot, too?'

'I enjoy books about history the most, but I have Mr Green from Newgate Street deliver what he feels worthy from his publishing business and some of those different books have been most enlightening.'

Adelia remembered Simeon had been carrying a book the other night when he had awoken her from her nightmares. Perhaps he slept as badly as she did?

She was about to ask him more when a group of men and women approached and their conversation faltered. She recognised Miss Rebecca Winston and her heart sank, for she was a friend of Mrs Trenwith.

'Mr Morgan, how good it is to finally meet you.' The tall man spoke first. 'I am Frank Winston and this is my wife, Penelope, and my sister, Rebecca Winston.' His glance came across to Adelia. 'I met Miss Worthington at the Thackerays' ball in January.'

'Mrs Morgan now.' Simeon's firm voice broke into the silence.

'Of course. Please forgive me.'

Rebecca Winston took over from her brother. 'It seems you have had a busy time since leaving London, Mrs Morgan. I suppose you are aware that the hearts of half of the male population of the *ton* were broken with loss when you left?'

Laughter rang around the group. She had departed under a dark cloud with every suitor withdrawing his hand from the game of marriage and well they would know it.

Straightening her spine, she reached for fortitude and smiled politely. 'I remember you as a woman with her own large set of admirers, Miss Winston, and as the central point in any group.' The words almost stuck in her throat, but Adelia knew that to keep the possibilities of Simeon's dreams alive she would need to be extremely diplomatic here. 'I have also long admired the cut of your beautiful gowns.'

The small silence was charged, but Adelia could feel the change in the atmosphere. Now Rebecca Winston was smiling in truth and she had moved back a little as though to allow her some space.

'Well, that is very kind of you to say so and, in truth, Rodney Anstruther was always a bit of a prig right from the time he was a child. I am sure you were well within your rights to admonish him with your umbrella.'

Adelia shook her head. 'No, that was a mistake I do regret. I would simply walk away from him next time.'

She didn't elaborate exactly what it was she would walk away from and saw the faces opposite her imagining some inappropriate gesture on the part of Mr Anstruther. With Simeon at her side it was much easier to partake in this social discourse because she did not feel so alone. He looked strong and real beside her, a man who might simply laugh at the small stupidities of society because he was trying to mould a better future for everyone, rich and poor alike.

She moved towards him just a little, liking the way her arm brushed his.

If he felt her there he made no sign of it, but then he did not pull away, either. Rebecca Winston was now practising her wiles on him with her fluttering eyelashes and a pattern of speech that was so patently false.

'I hear you have just bought a large piece of land on the river at Richmond, Mr Morgan. It is by far the prettiest area in all of London, I have always said, with the trees and the birdsong and the peacefulness. What sort of a house do you plan to build there?'

'A sturdy one, Miss Winston...'

'Oh, call me Rebecca, please. With the sliding roles of the aristocracy and the merchants in society the formalities have long since disappeared, and perhaps it is for the best.'

Her tone plainly said that such a turnabout was undesirable and unwelcomed. Adelia thought this conversation was one that Simeon must have had time and time again in his quest for equality, but he did not flinch in the slightest as he gave her his reply.

'I imagine everyone is scrambling for purchase in this new world and Lord Grey has been most kind to give me a hand up.'

His response was as veiled as her own, the truth hidden somewhere under his words. This was how he had survived, thrived even, when the old vanguard had caught the whiff of his unexpected triumphs and unhidden ambitions. By allowing them gratitude and making less of himself he remained untouched.

She wished she'd had the wit to recognise such a strategy when she had endured her seemingly endless Season six months before. The ridiculous expectations of making the most advantageous marriage might have been less exasperating had she simply laughed at it or played along and then left to be exactly as she had been.

'Where was it that you met your wife, Mr Morgan?' Frank Winston asked this question, and Adelia waited for his answer.

'At my town house in Carlton House Terrace. It was a small and informal family gathering.'

Very small, she thought and swallowed down guilt.

'You knew the Viscount, then?' Frank looked surprised.

'Briefly.'

'The rumours were that Worthington offered you Athelridge Hall as a part of the dowry.'

'In truth, the land meant little for it was his daughter I was far more interested in.'

A new streak of shock ran through Adelia as she looked over at him, his eyes catching hers properly for the first time tonight and blazing in memory, making the time thin between then and now.

His mouth at her breast, the heat of him beguiling, his skin dark against the candlelight, hair long and loose. An image that only they could share and shocking in the present moment.

'So when we finally gave our troths our wedding could not come soon enough.'

The spell was broken, fractured into pieces falling out of shape, jagged bits of half-lies. The act of a man who used tonight as a show and an opportunity. She was no more than a prop. She looked away. There was still dinner to get through and presumably some dancing as well and she was pleased when they were called to the table, Lord Grey at her elbow and Lady Grey at Simeon's.

Simeon.

She had started referring to him by his Christian name just to herself and it felt right. She hoped he would be seated next to her or somewhere near at least and as he came to stand behind the chair to her left she was grateful. A charade it might be, but at least she understood the rules of it and she knew he would never deliberately harm her.

Chapter Eight

Hell, Simeon thought, this was far harder to get through than he could have imagined and Adelia looked as if she, too, was finding the whole thing exhausting.

Sitting, he poured out wine from the bottle before them and raised his glass to her.

'Thank you.'

He wanted to say more for she had been the essence of a perfect wife with her conciliatory demeanour and her beautiful smile. She had beaten them at their own game again and again with diplomacy, refinement, grace and tact. Just as she had promised him when she'd made him an offer of marriage.

'You are welcome.'

The woman Rebecca Winston was sitting too close on his other side, her leg touching his own until he had moved away. She smelt of some strong perfume that he disliked. Frank Winston glowered at him and Simeon knew that he was trying to protect his sister from the taint of trade that even a fortune could not remove. Further along the table, two other men were looking at Adelia as if she was the answer to every male's prayer ever uttered and Simeon could well see why.

Under the lights her hair took on colours he had not noticed before and the brilliant hue of her eyes exactly matched the emerald earrings she wore. With the sort of admiration that swirled around her from all the men present he wondered again at her need to approach him for the role of husband. Athelridge Hall was a card in his pocket, but he knew, even though she had no fortune, she could have made the match of the year should she have wanted to and he certainly was not that.

Her hand lay on the table between them, a long white glove showing off the small and delicate shape. He suddenly felt tired by it all, the past, the present, the striving, the uncertainty. He was only here to make sure that the lines of communication for people who were often voiceless were left open. A quiet pilgrimage that might give back a little to the communities that had been his once, all those years ago, places of desperation and bleakness.

His uncle had a hand in this, too, a self-made man who had held the principles of charity and philanthropy as guiding goals and believed very firmly in the notion of one man being able to make a difference.

Jamie Morgan would have liked his wife, he thought, just as he had loathed Susan Downing with her melancholy and her unending neediness. He watched Adelia as she chatted with those across the table from her, a stream of interesting conversation, but words that gave nothing at all of herself away. He'd learnt the knack of such dialogue when he had first come into the field of investments, for his beginnings in business were both forced and unnatural. It was only when he had begun to understand his true direction and the need for diplomacy to achieve it that he'd seen the requirement to be largely formal and undisputedly impersonal. A different man, the rough edges softened by detachment, the anger inside made more pliable by his new ability to pretend, his accent carefully bland and minutely copied from those men of society whom he'd had business with.

As if aware of his silence Adelia turned to him and smiled, a quietly worded question falling into the space between them.

'Lord Grey's brother was just saying that any new railway needs an Act of Parliament passed to begin the works. Is that correct?'

'He's right. They do not come cheap, either, and any opposition can effectively prevent construction.'

'Who would oppose such a thing when it helps so many people?'

'Canal companies who are unable or unwilling to upgrade their facilities to compete with railways, for one, and they use their political power effectively.'

'And what happens then?'

'Purchasing a large share of the canal companies is a good solution. It neutralises intent.'

'My goodness, that seems very wrong to have to buy into such corruption.'

He laughed. 'The world of business has its shadows, Adelia.'

'Do you wish it didn't?'

He felt his heart beat in his throat, felt the shame that had so often accompanied such transactions.

'I have not made a fortune by being only

black or white, but at the end of the day there are sacrifices that are probably worthwhile.'

Her expression was puzzled. 'I was just speaking with Lord Grey's brother and he sees you as a pioneer in the field and one of the few men who has not traded his soul for gain.'

'Then I hope Grey feels the same way about me.'

'Even if it is not true?'

'Even then.'

'Are you as honest with others as you are with me, Mr Morgan?'

'Simeon,' he qualified. 'And, no.'

Her dimples surprised him. 'Then I am glad for it.'

'What of you, Adelia? Were there other times, apart from the circumstances surrounding our marriage, when you hawked your principals for an end result, when you have sold lies for expediency?'

'Yes.'

'But you will not tell me?'

'We are at a dinner party, Mr Morgan, fighting for your future. It is better, I think, to concentrate on one thing at a time.'

'You do that well, I think.'

'Pardon?'

'Beguile others into believing anything you want them to.'

'That could be taken as an insult.'

He leaned forward and lifted her hand, the glove covering skin, the whiteness slender. He felt her warmth through the fabric. 'But it was not meant to be. I'm impressed by your talent in making small talk.'

'The building blocks of relationships,' she shot back. 'The mortar between bricks.'

'It's a game I am poor at. One day I will tell you why.'

This time she turned into him, and he felt her thigh full up against his own beneath the table.

'Everyone here is in awe of your unending capacity to make good decisions in business. I doubt high marks for small talk have a huge importance on any list of financial largesse.'

'Yet these are the last of the railway lines that I shall build. I might even sell those I already have.'

He could not believe he had said that to her, here in a room full of his competitors. But if his unending capacity for sound financial decisions were to continue, he knew that the cloud of ruin was already inherent in the proliferation of existing lines and the lack of government regulation over them.

'You wish to leave these lords to their own game, then?'

He laughed. 'No, I want to beat them all at it.'

'Lofty goals?'

'But very attainable.'

'Are you always so certain in your strategies?'

'I am,' he returned and for a moment he wondered if he was talking about business or about her.

The fellow next to Adelia turned and took her attention and as Simeon looked across the table he saw Winston raise his glass and speak.

'Here's to you, Mr Morgan, and to the future of the railway.'

His own glass was in hand, the crystal catching the light and sending a rainbow across the plate before him.

'The future,' he repeated and knew that what was to come did not belong in the shares of iron tracks or the frenzied bubbles of speculative purchasers driving the price so high that it could only collapse.

He'd build this part of the system and then he'd get out.

Nothing lasted for ever. Not love. Not hope and not luck. And certainly not marriage.

And if Adelia was helping him tonight, then tomorrow she would undoubtedly be gone, back to her beloved Athelridge Hall and away from the city. Away from him.

That thought disturbed Simeon, for he would have enjoyed showing her his London, a place of river walks and gardens and beautiful buildings. Richmond and the new piece of land came to mind, but he shoved that thought away. Adelia was as skilled as he was at pretending, but it still did not make anything true.

He was suddenly aware that Grey at one end of the table was watching him and he worried about the calculation in his wily old eyes. It was just as well that Lord Grey had no notion as to what had just been said between him and Adelia. Again he felt a tremor of guilt run through him.

Then Lord Grey rang his knife against his crystal glass and everyone stopped speaking.

'I have an announcement,' he said, his voice as serious as Simeon had ever heard it. Lady Grey was smiling, giving the impression that she already knew what it was her husband might say. 'I want to tell you all that Mr Simeon Morgan will be my partner on the next railway project in the north.'

Simeon had not expected such a public promise, and Adelia at his side placed her hand across his and he felt her grip tighten.

'Congratulations.' Her voice was small and quiet. 'A victory of sorts, at least?'

He understood what she meant and was grateful, but having achieved everything he had set out to do, all he wanted now was to take his wife home. Lord Grey, however, was not quite finished.

'Tonight Mr Morgan and his new bride celebrate only a few weeks of married life together and I would like to give them some advice. Be honest and be adaptable, for without either your union will wither. Celebrate the things that make you different as well as all the things in which you are alike.'

Simeon tipped his head in thanks and Adelia's dimples caught the light from the chandelier above them, sending shadows across her cheeks.

It seemed that an answer was expected so he stood. 'We will both take your advice to heart, Lord Grey, and we thank you for the good wishes. With a marriage as successful and long as your own we can only benefit from such insightful guidance.' He raised his glass. 'So here's to longevity and triumph.' He deliberately left out love.

Dancing followed the dinner and once the meal was cleared away a small group of musicians set themselves up at the head of the room. Adelia was excited about the prospect, but Simeon looked less than enthusiastic.

'Do you enjoy a twirl, Mr Morgan?'

'I do not, Mrs Morgan.'

This was a new retort, for more normally he gave her back her Christian name or insisted she use his.

'But you will ask me for a waltz?'

His frown deepened. 'My education did not extend to the fine and intricate arts of dancing.'

'But you do know the steps?'

He remained silent.

'You don't?' Amazement filled her. Here was something she might teach him. 'It would be more than easy if you just follow my lead.'

He looked horrified, but out of the corner of her eye she saw Rebecca Winston advancing on him with that particular look of a predatory female and she knew Simeon had seen her, too. With the first strains of music beginning, she literally gave him no choice, her hand on his arm as she urged him forward.

Just for a moment she wanted him to know that in all of the abrasive weeks leading up to the wedding and all the silence after that there might be something they could now share in a way that was pleasant. A dance. Touching. Listening to the music and feeling it.

This evening had showed her the sort of man that Simeon Morgan was: clever, strong and himself. He did not pretend a knowledge about the many odd mannerisms of society, but he didn't let it worry him, either. He'd been honest about his dancing finesse and yet he still allowed her to lead him to the floor as if being shown how to do something was another challenge he would rise to.

She'd hated each and every dance she had been made to stand up for during her Season, the wandering hands, the senseless conversations, the prying eyes all around. She had been tongue-tied by the very notion of the marriage mart, the expectations and the disappointment. Marriage to Simeon had never felt boring. He was a man who said what he felt and meant what he said. No guesswork. No covert hidden agenda. He had not wanted to marry her and he had never pretended otherwise. But his conversation was stimulating and worthy. He listened to her opinions as no one else ever had and gave her back a logical explanation of his own beliefs and ideas. He did not sweeten the taste of disagreement with lies.

So here now she wanted to say thank-you, to pay back a tiny bit of his generosity in the care he had given her family whom he had very little reason to like.

Her fingers came into his and she placed his other hand on her left shoulder blade.

'The waltz is a smooth dance, travelling in a line and characterised primarily by its rise and fall action. Your shoulders move parallel with the floor and not up and down and your head looks over my right shoulder. Then it's just counting. We stand a little bit sideways from each other, like this.' She placed her feet so that his left foot came between her own. 'Then we count. *One* two three, *two* two three, *three* two three, *four* two three. And that is it, really.'

She stopped and with their faces only inches away from each other a dislocation assailed her. They had been like this when first they had met, the heat around them, the forbidden closeness, the link of flesh and desire and need.

Now they were fully clothed and in a room crowded with others and yet it was as if they were alone, only them, the musicians in the background, the slick beat of their bodies counting time, both in the fall and in the rise. The dance of love. She blushed and if he saw he made no comment. She could see him measuring out the beat stiff with concentration and trying to understand it exactly. After a moment he relaxed, his breath slowing and the grip of his hand less rigid.

'You are doing well.' She felt she should say something as the silence between them lengthened and when he smiled at her she understood that the beauty in him was undeniably potent. The beauty of a man who knew who he was and did not pretend to be who he wasn't.

'At least I have not yet tripped you up.'

'I wish you could have danced with me during my endless Season.'

It was a boldness to say so and she knew she had strayed across a boundary, yet she could not take it back, could not retract that which she honestly thought with all her heart.

The gold in his eyes sharpened and focused. 'I am certain you would have refused me, Adelia. Is it not said that every debutante who arrives in society for the Season is after a title from some ancient family?'

She shook her head. 'I was simply after a real conversation and a man who could look me in the face and was not overcome by what he saw.'

He frowned and his grip tightened on her back. 'You think I am immune to the way you look?'

She did not know quite how to answer this without sounding vain. 'Well, unlike all my other suitors, you have never mentioned my beauty.'

'You wanted me to?' The humour was back, threaded through his query.

'No. I was glad when you didn't.'

'But you think I do not notice it?'

'Do you?' Her heart began to speed up. She could hear and feel the beat of it in her throat and knew that he would, too.

'When people smile, Adelia, everyone is beautiful.'

His answer was so unexpected she began to laugh.

'You think I do not smile enough?'

'I think it is good to finally see you happy.'

And she was, there in his arms, the music swelling and their steps gaining in confidence. She wished the dance might have gone on for ever but it didn't, the last notes of the music fading into silence.

Lord Grey joined them with his wife.

'I remember seeing you at some of the events from last Season, Mrs Morgan. You never looked as cheerful as you do now.'

His statement was not said in any other way than as a passing reference and Adelia was pleased that he seemed to require no true answer. Still, she saw Simeon take note of the words.

'We are having a country gathering in three weeks at our estate in Kent, Mr Morgan. My wife and I wondered if you both might also like to join us there.'

A further invitation. Simeon answered for her.

'That is kind of you to ask, but in the next few days I am going to the north for a month and so it is unfortunately impossible.'

All the gladness left Adelia in one breath. Of

course he would not want to do this again, especially after he had just concluded the business
concerning the new railway tracks to his satisfaction. No, after tomorrow she would be once
more back at Athelridge Hall with her mother
and sister and all this would be only a memory.

An inconvenient wife and a marriage forced
upon him. She wondered again where the red-
headed beauty who had come to their wedding
was now. Waiting for him in some luxurious
bed, no doubt, sultry and sensual? Passing the
hours until her lover was back from complet-
ing his duties with an unwanted bride and then
laughing about it with him.

She pasted a smile across her face and
thought she had never had such a night of ups
and downs.

Adelia looked crestfallen at his reply and he
could not understand why that should be. She
had stipulated precisely that what she wanted
was a sham of a marriage and nothing more,
though as he had held her in the waltz he had
thought perhaps things were changing. In the
dance he had wanted to keep holding her in
his arms, the sweet touch of her a closeness he
had not felt in a very long time.

The invitation from Lord Grey and his wife for them to attend another social occasion had surprised him, though he understood why people had warmed to Adelia.

She was interesting. She listened well and her conversation was knowledgeable and sensible. When she had showed him the steps of the waltz he had understood for the first time exactly what his feet and body should be doing. Before tonight he would never have attempted such a thing in a room full of people.

Her dimples had been easily seen and he was glad of it. A beautiful woman, her father's poor character harder and harder to see in her the more he got to know her.

He wanted to ask her why she had been so unbending in her insistence on a marriage between them. He wanted to know that closeness he had experienced the first time he'd met her and felt her response to him, but Grey was asking him a question and it brought him back to the moment.

'You know you are a lucky man, Simeon? I thought that Adelia Worthington was one of the finest girls of the Season and I was right. You suit each other and I wish you all the best in the world.'

* * *

The carriage ride home was a silent one, the unsettling realisation of his imminent departure to the north leaving her stranded. If Simeon journeyed from London tomorrow for the north and sent her home to Athelridge Hall, then there was no hope for them and yet she could hardly demand it be otherwise.

He was quiet in his corner of the conveyance, street lights blinking on his face as they passed them by, his expression distant and aloof until a sudden lunge of the horses jolted the carriage and threw her along the seat, the shout of the drivers loud. As if by magic Simeon was beside her, his arm tethering her to the leather, protecting her, making certain she was safe.

'It's all right. I think we missed whatever it was the driver did his best to avoid.'

Glancing outside, he banged on the roof. Within a few seconds the horses pulled up and the driver came to the door.

'It were a pedestrian, sir. He walked straight out in front of us and if we had not swerved then God knows what might have happened. A drunk, probably, with little sense but a lot of luck.'

'Very well, Kennedy.' Simeon's voice was gruff. 'Just get us home safely.'

'I will do, sir.'

In the next second the driver was gone and the carriage went on at a much diminished speed. Simeon made no move to return to his former seat, but stayed beside her.

'You were more than helpful tonight, Adelia.'

Surprise made her look at him. He was not a man adept at using flattery, so it certainly was not an empty truth.

'A useful thing, then, ancestry?'

He smiled. 'I do not just attach my compliment to the completion of any business transaction, I assure you. I meant it sincerely.'

She frowned because he seemed different and she did not wish to be disappointed again if she was interpreting things wrongly. 'There is no one to observe us here, Mr Morgan. I absolve you from any pretension.'

'You think that is all tonight was?'

Adelia stiffened. 'I don't know what you mean.'

'Do you not?'

He turned then so that there was barely any space between them, his hand touching her arm. Skin to skin.

'When you came to me that first night I thought you might have been an angel sent down by a celestial being. I was sick with the fever, you see, and so…' He gathered his words and went on. 'When you told me you were your father's daughter I imagined he might have come along with you and would jump out unannounced and insist on reprisal.'

'He might well have done so had he still been alive.'

'When I asked you to go away, you didn't. Why not?'

'I felt safe with you until you said you pitied me…'

'I still do.'

She removed her hand.

'I pitied you for the father you had, for his lack of scruples and for his stupidity. No man should blow his brains out in front of his child.'

'Yet you didn't know he had, then.'

'I knew you had fresh bruises all over your arms and neck. I knew you were scared. I knew that in all your demands there lay secrets and that Lionel Worthington was one of them.'

'You asked me once if I had killed him.'

'I believed you might have until last night when you told me the truth.'

'Yet you brought me to London and found me a gown…'

'People sometimes kill for reasons that do have merit, Adelia, it's not always cut and dried.'

'So why did you give me the benefit of the doubt?'

'Because I have walked among killers and you did not fit the mould.'

'In your past? In the childhood you don't speak of and the one which everyone else does? That is how you know them? These killers?'

'You are not the only one who has ever considered taking revenge, Adelia, for the sins committed against you.'

Her ire dropped away into shock. They were so different and yet there was so much in them that was the same.

Pity.

It was a word with far more meaning in it than she had first considered.

'Who was your father, then?' Her question came without thought.

'A man who decided to leave my mother almost at the same time as I was born. A weak man of no principle and little sense.'

'And you never saw him again?'

'Unfortunately I did on and off over the first five years of my life. Neil Finnegan came back on occasions to steal from my mother and to beat us up.'

'So you took your mother's name?'

'Not quite.' He didn't elaborate further as he turned to her and she felt the broken thing inside him reaching out, bringing her in, his mouth coming down, the hardness in him as apparent as the shame.

This was no easy quiet kiss, but a brand, stamping his need, imprinting her with the force of his want. A kiss that spoke of harshness and terror, but also of passion barely bridled, loosened with his confession and riding on the edge of lust.

Adelia could have broken away and refused him, but she did not. All resistance faded into feeling, his tongue, his lips, his hands drawing her closer, her head tipped up to pleasure and the air between them shared.

'Open for me, Lia.'

Whispered words, urging her to comply, and she did, the shadows of night and quietness giving way to a red-hot roar of hunger as well as a deep-set ache, inexplicable and potent.

Entwined in need, all the past that had shattered him once now put back together in desire.

She wanted to heal him, make him whole, for tonight his strength and honour had been easy to see, the power of him not in entitlement or possessions, but in intelligence and honesty.

He was like no one else she had ever met and yet he was a stranger, drawn in outline, waiting to be filled in. Her husband by law, but unfamiliar in every other single way that mattered.

Deepening the kiss, he came in at another angle, searching, telling her wordlessly of all that he wanted. Her breath shivered and another wave of craving sent her spinning into his centre, no space between them, no hidden and veiled purpose.

Only him. Only her. Fused by longing. His hands captured her hair and pulled her back, tasting her throat now and the skin above the lace in her low bodice. No quiet savouring, either, but a fervent and fierce proximity making her nipples harden.

He was a master at sensation, neither green fumbling boy nor arrogant lord, but masculine and true and heart wrenching. She felt his thumb there, felt the discovery and then the consequence.

Heaven. Breathless. Drawn in. Like iron filings to a magnet, his power both nameless and sightless, though shock engulfed her as the driver called the horses to a halt and the light from the street lamp in front of his town house flooded inside the carriage.

Exposed. Caught in disbelief. Her lips felt wet, swollen and bruised even as she wiped them. How could he do this as easily as he had done last time? It was as if he touched her and her wits deserted her, the woman who remained one she had no familiarity with. Even now she wanted him, with a brutal and wild intensity.

Her shaking fingers caught her hair and twisted it back into the collar of her cloak, anchoring the errant curls even as he swore.

'Damn.'

Only that word in the silence of the night, no explanation of what any of this meant. For them.

Inside the town house, Simeon asked her if she would join him in the front salon. Unable to refuse, she followed him in and watched as he shut the door. He stood by the window, looking out at the street as he often did. It had begun to rain and the glass was blurred, but the evening was still warm despite the early autumn.

'This marriage of ours...' he stated at last as he turned and then stopped as if fighting to find the right words. 'What is it exactly you want from me, Adelia?'

A baldly stated question full of frustration and accusation. There was nothing in his tone that suggested reconciliation or appeasement or any of the emotions she'd felt a few moments earlier. It was as if the kiss between them had only angered him further, heightening differences, widening contrasts.

'You insisted on a contract of marriage that was false and you sealed it publicly with your lies. Yet now...' He compressed his lips tightly and laid his hands on the mantel behind him, body bent. 'The kiss in the carriage, was that just a pretence, too?'

She shook her head because she could not speak.

'Then who is the Honourable Alexander Thompson? To you?'

Her world caved in, like a pack of cards

badly formed, falling, falling until there was nothing left.

'He is only a friend.'

'A friend who loves you? A friend who is more than a friend? A friend who you pay handsomely for "*labour*" as seen in the ledgers Peter Shelman shows me?'

Shock made it hard to breathe.

'How did you know about him…?' She realised that was the wrong question to ask the minute she had done so.

'So you don't deny it? You stand there with his heart in your hands and dare to kiss me?'

'No. It is not like that at all.'

'Then how is it? Tell me how it is, Adelia. Help me to understand.'

'He was just a friend who taught me things.'

'Things like who to marry in order to continue a relationship with him? If that is the case, you picked the wrong man in me and I hope like hell that you know it.'

The dizzying horror made her feel sick. All he said was the truth in the way that he would interpret it.

'Ever since you came into my life you have lied and deceived me and cheated to get what you wanted. You have shown me you are a woman who is every bit as devious as her father.'

She tried to slap him then, in her distress, and felt his hand tighten on her own in response.

'Don't make me hate you again, Adelia. Not after tonight.'

The ground was torn out from beneath her feet. If she had been braver, she might have spoken up for the kiss, for the dance, for the safety. But her courage had completely deserted her and lay shattered at her feet in tiny bits of shame. She stayed quiet because any admission would undo her.

'I think that you are a woman who clings to the best chance for herself and is able to turn facts on their heads with an ease that is disturbing. I also think you could probably give the best courtesans in London a run for their money with your expertise in kissing.'

She blushed and hated herself for doing so.

'Then if pretence is a skill, Mr Morgan, you are equally as good in the art as I am.'

He moved at that. 'Really?' One finger carefully traced its way down her cheek across her throat and on to the flesh above her bodice. She felt her skin raise in response. 'In my experience, pretence does not usually look like this.'

He brushed his hand across her lips like a feather, barely there. Breathing out, she tipped her head back and waited and when his lips came down across her own she shut her eyes and only felt, shock burning its way through her body, warming all the coldness that had been there for ever.

She couldn't stop him even despite the words, the accusations, the anger. This was more than all of that put together and if lust could make her feel complete then who was she to bring it to a halt? Simeon would never love her, she knew that, or trust her, but this was another language entirely and one which, apparently, they both could speak fluently.

Her hand cradled his neck and she leant in, wanting what he offered with every fibre of her being. She knew that she had him when his breath hitched in surrender, only the two of them in a world of silence.

It was unlike any kiss he had given her before because this one held an element of desperation, an anchor offering a safe harbour for this small piece of time, caught to each other by consequence just before a storm.

He did not hold back as he pushed her up against the wall, his tongue searching her mouth and widening the kiss, a yearning rolling across her in a rhythm that was as old as time.

Love me. Want me. Hold me. Know me.

His knee came in hard between her legs, only the silk of her dress a flimsy barrier. A new assault that conjured up other feelings, stronger ones even as he broke away and laid his forehead against her own, breathing with difficulty, panting in want, hands splayed on each side of her, pushed to the limit.

'This is not a pretence, Adelia. At least admit that.'

'Not a…pretence.'

It was all she could say as the tears began to roll down her cheeks, splattering against the coffee-coloured silk and darkening the fabric.

If he had wanted her again, he could have simply leant in and she would have followed him anywhere.

But he didn't.

Stepping away, he stayed still, the air that had been warm between them becoming colder.

'When the truth is something that you might like to give me, then I will be here to listen.'

Then he was gone.

Immobile, she balanced herself against the wall, finding her equilibrium again in all that had been lost. And yet in what had been lost there was also that which had been gained. Knowledge. Understanding. When Alexander had kissed her all she had felt was the wrongness of it and in the wandering hands of other suitors all she remembered feeling was distaste.

Simeon's caresses were totally different, the heat inside her still clenching in waves around her body. She wanted what she imagined might come next; she wanted a true intimacy and all the hours in the world to discover his body. She wanted him to carry her to his bed and show her that which he had learnt in a lifetime encompassing both the easy and the hard.

She wondered who had told him of her friendship with Alexander and hoped with all her heart that it was not her mother who had betrayed her. She cursed the money she had allowed him out of guilt and concern and vowed there would be no more.

If she could save this marriage, she would be

lucky. If she couldn't, she did not quite know what might happen to her.

Simeon pulled off his necktie and flicked off his boots. His jacket and waistcoat came next. Without the restriction of these things he began to move more easily, the choking feeling in his throat reducing back into a shadow.

He wanted her. He wanted Adelia Hermione Josephine Bennett Morgan with an ache that utterly consumed him. He wanted to kiss her and undress her and bring her to his bed where he could enjoy her for the whole night piece by little piece. He was not a refined lord who might take a small offering, though. No, he desired her wholeness in a raw and visceral way. Just one simple kiss had left him stunned and confounded and at odds with what to do next.

He should send her back to Athelridge Hall on the morrow and depart for the north, but he knew that he would not. He cursed ever hearing the name of Alexander Thompson and he cursed Theodora Wainwright for placing the doubt into his head in the first place.

Adelia's reaction to hearing the gossip about her and Thompson had not been quite the one he'd expected. The blood had drained from her face and her hands had been shaking.

Everything had changed on him. Work. Home. Life. It had all been upended in a startling and unsettling way, the quiet certainty of his future worn down by ambiguity.

For so long now he had beaten the path of great ambition and never stopped, venturing always onwards and upwards just as his mother's uncle had directed him.

James Morgan. His saviour.

He shook his head and refused the pain that always came at the thought of his great-uncle's death. The only adult in his life who had ever cared for him and had showed it day after day, year after year. Not for profit or evil, not for duty either, but only for love.

His true father had frequently bashed him up, his other 'fathers' had wanted darker, painful things from him, but Jamie Morgan had only ever wanted what was best for him.

Crossing the room, he looked into the mirror at himself. Did he appear different after kissing his wife? Did the hope show in his eyes or on his lips? Did the disappointment knowing about Alexander Thompson lay scrawled in places anyone might notice?

Tomorrow Flora and her new governess would be back in London after an overnight stay with Catherine's sister. Even though she'd never live with her aunt, Simeon had wanted Flora to feel connected to her only relative and Catherine's sister had finally agreed to a short visit. Would Adelia be appalled to have the child of her father's mistress in residence? He hoped she had no knowledge of the liaison, but a sixth sense told him she probably did. She did not act like a woman who missed much.

He sat down and laid his head back against the headrest of the chair by the window. From here he could see trees and beautiful buildings, a far cry from the squalid shambles of his boyhood.

He thought of his confession to Adelia at the dinner about selling all the railway routes he now owned. He wanted a simpler life. He wanted to build on the river at Richmond and just stop. He wanted to smell the flowers and hear the birdsong and know the peace of a house that would be his for ever.

For ever.

Two words that hadn't been part of any vocabulary of his until now.

Another change. A further difference she'd made to him.

He needed to get to know Adelia properly, without judgement from anyone else and without discrimination. She was his wife. She was also the only woman he had ever kissed who made him feel…right.

His secrets were a thousand times worse than anything he had discovered about her past, so why could he not put it behind him and move forward?

That reflection was comforting, as was the thought of her being here, in his house, in the yellow room upstairs overlooking the street. She was safe and cared for, she was warm and protected and just for this moment it was enough.

Chapter Nine

The voice of a small child brought Adelia downstairs around mid-morning to find the same little girl standing in the entrance hall who she had seen the first time she had come here.

'Hello.'

Dark eyes turned towards Adelia and the girl frowned.

'I know you, from before?'

'You do. My name is Adelia and I am married to Mr Morgan.'

'His wife?' Worry puckered her mouth. 'But…'

She had no time to say more as another woman joined them, a young plump woman with kind eyes.

'I wondered where you had gone, Miss Flora, until I heard you speaking.'

Giving the same introduction as she had to the child, Adelia waited.

'I am Maureen Brown, Miss Flora's governess, ma'am. We have arrived from the south of London just now after a night with Flora's aunt. But it is good to be home again. Shall we find your family, Miss Flora, and see what they have all been doing while we were away?'

Her family? Home? Here?

She'd woken this morning with the worry of being sent away summarily, only to find her husband had gone out and would not be back again until after luncheon. Was this child his? She wanted to kneel down and ask just who the little girl's mother was, but of course she could not do that.

Instead, she straightened and watched as they disappeared into the large sprawling house, wondering if perhaps Simeon had slipped back unnoticed and was in his library or office, keeping well out of her way.

She caught her reflection in the mirror as she turned. There were large dark circles beneath her eyes from a lack of sleep and she looked far from her best. She had dragged on an old dress from her meagre belongings and she now tried to smooth down the creases, but the mid-blue fabric seemed to have a mind of its own and bounced back into wrinkles. Even the governess she had just met looked more fashionable than she did.

This marriage was turning out exactly opposite to the way she had imagined it would. She'd thought that they would barely see each other and instead had been thrown into an emotional turmoil, one she was struggling to understand.

The trouble was she genuinely liked him, liked talking to him, liked his strength and honesty, liked the way he moved in society with such ease. He was not petty or bitter or resentful even though she had given him reason to be.

As she was thinking this Simeon walked in the front door. Unlike her, his clothes today were well ironed, and if his night had been restless there was no sign of it at all.

'I am glad to see you here, Adelia, because I need to talk to you. In the library, if you do not mind.'

She followed him in a new direction and to a part of the house she had not yet seen. His library was at the back of the property, its ceiling high and a set of doors running off into a surprisingly verdant garden.

'Take a seat.' He appeared distracted.

She chose an upright chair upholstered in plush red velvet.

'I take it you have met Miss Flora Rountree?'

'The little girl with the long dark hair? Yes. Though I met her the first time I came to your house, as well. She had a black eye then.'

'Which is precisely why I fired her first governess and employed a new one. I have also taken steps to ensure the unsuitable Mrs Wade will never look after another child.'

'She is your daughter?'

He shook his head. 'Her mother, Mrs Catherine Rountree, was a friend of mine and she entrusted Flora into my care after her death.'

'Mrs Catherine Rountree?' Adelia said the name out loud and knew suddenly why it was familiar.

'I see you know the name?' His tone held a question.

'She was my father's mistress.'

'He was also the one who killed her. Did you know that, as well? There was an accident a few months ago. Lionel Worthington was drunk and in a high temper and, after crashing their carriage, he left the scene, not even tarrying to see if Catherine was still alive. Which she wasn't.'

'And the child?'

'Was not with them, which was incredibly lucky, though I imagine she has heard things about what happened. She is a sullen little girl and inclined to melancholy.'

'And that is why she has been to stay with her aunt?'

He poured a drink for himself and offered her one. When she shook her head, he sat and took a sip of his own.

'I'd hoped her aunt might be persuaded to take an interest in Flora's welfare, but it seems she has enough children of her own to deal with and so has no inclination for such a task.'

'Which leaves you.'

'I have the space and the capital and the new governess, Miss Brown, seems amiable. It is only…' He stopped and looked at her.

'Last night you helped me at the dinner and I was more than grateful. I know it was not easy for either of us in the end, but I would like to put that behind us and move on. Are you agreeable to such a suggestion?'

'I am.'

'Then might I ask you for another favour, Adelia?'

She nodded.

'Could you be kind to the child and take her under your wing? She needs someone more permanent, I think, and as my wife…'

He left the rest unsaid, lying there exposed.

Permanent. When she had expected this morning to be packed up summarily and sent back to Athelridge Hall.

'I know as a man that I can never be exactly what a little girl might need.'

'The child's mother knew you could be trusted. She knew you were a man who always kept your word. She knew you were not someone who would let her down. That is enough in my book.'

With care, she stood and faced him directly.

'When you did not tell the world about my ill-conceived visit alone to your town house that first night I knew you were honourable. I once told you that I would have married anyone with the deeds to Athelridge Hall in their pockets, but that was not quite the truth. My father had said that your honour would be the ruin of you and I remembered his praise of you, for he seldom allowed anyone a compliment.'

'Including you?'

'This conversation is not about me, Mr Morgan. It is about a child to whom you have given a home and now you want her to feel as if she belongs. I can help with that.'

'I would be grateful.' Rifling through his desk, he came up with a letter and handed it over. 'This came for you first thing this morning from your friend, Mr Thompson. I give it to you, Adelia, with the warning that I should not like to be cuckolded, for any reason and with any man.'

'You will not be.' With care, she tucked the letter into her pocket. 'I promised you my loyalty and I meant it.'

'Good to know.'

She was glad he said no more. A cut and dried man. A man who would not whine on about his problems like her father had. As she looked around the room, her eyes touched on a portrait behind his desk of an older man with dark hair and a smile.

'My uncle,' he said suddenly. 'He died six years ago.'

'The one who took you in? You look like him.'

'He was actually my mother's uncle.'

'But you took his name?' She saw the words on the plate beneath—'James Morgan' engraved into gold, the dates of his birth and death under that.

'Family has to be earned, I think. My mother never quite got the trick of it.'

'In truth, I don't think my parents did, either.'

'Your father hurt Flora.' He said this quietly, almost in a whisper.

New words. New worries.

'How?'

'He tried to strangle her. Catherine walked in just in time. I think it is why she died a matter of days later. Lionel Worthington wanted no one else to know what he had tried to do, but she had already written to me. Did he ever hurt you that way?'

'Often. He hurt Charlotte, too, and because she was so much smaller than I was it was up to me to stop him.'

'How?'

'In the daytime I kept her with me and in the night… I ceased sleeping in my room and sat in hers whenever he was home. He knew why I did it.'

'You had many bruises on your skin the first time I saw you.'

'I told you when he died I was relieved and I meant it. The only person in my family who truly shed a tear after his death was Mama, but then she had only ever imagined the good in him.'

'Was there any?'

'None. He was a cheat and he was cruel. I used to hope my mother might tell me that he was not, in truth, my real father and that she had enjoyed another lover in Scotland who was kind and good and honourable. But of course she didn't.' Looking up, she smiled at him, there through the afternoon light, his eyes a soft gold and his hair very dark. 'I've never told anyone that before.'

'All children with imperfect parents hold that dream, Adelia.'

'Do you think Flora will recover?' Adelia could not imagine all the horrors the little girl had been through.

Simeon leant back and though he looked relaxed, Adelia could tell that he wasn't.

'I do because she has to. Sometimes there is no way to look back and live. You have to go forward.'

He was speaking of himself, she knew it. He was talking of his childhood and allowing her a window into it and the quiet tone he spoke in belied another truth. What had happened to him? What demons sat upon his shoulders? Something told her that both she, her sister and Flora had got off lightly compared to his trials. It was there on his face, in the ghost of memories and fury.

'I sent your father a letter after hearing of what he had done to Flora. I threatened him with death if I ever saw him near the child again. I followed it up later with a visit to him and he killed himself soon afterwards. The letter eventually ended up in Catherine's effects, but I don't know whether he took it home first and you read it or not, but if you did, I wanted to explain it.'

'Because you thought I might blame you?'

'After our conversation today I rather think you would be more likely to thank me, but you never know. Generally, in business, I always find the truth to be valuable.'

'And is this what this is? Business?'

'Isn't it?'

The room seemed smaller, the air lessened.

She suddenly desperately needed to know the answer to her next question.

'Is Flora my father's daughter, Simeon?'

'No. Her father was a man Catherine Rountree married in Manchester eight years ago. He died shortly after she gave birth to Flora.'

'Would you have killed my papa if he had not heeded your warnings about Flora?'

'Without a doubt.'

She believed him and was glad. She had never felt this way with anyone before, this breathless gravity. She had never known what the true power of loving someone was until she had been in his company.

Love.

The word made her stand abruptly lest he suddenly see it clearly written on her face.

'I will help you with Flora in any way you see fit. You just have to ask.' Then she turned on her heel and rushed out of the library.

In her own room a few moments later, she sat down on her bed, her head in her hands. My God. She loved him. She did. She loved Simeon with all her heart and soul and she knew exactly why. He was honourable and clever and honest and direct. It had nothing to do with his money or his possessions or the fact that as a self-made man he stood at the helm of business.

She had tricked a saint into marriage.

That thought made her smile because he would hardly see himself as that. But to her...

Another thought struck. How was she to go on from here? She had never felt this way before and she could already sense a difference in herself. A joy. A gratitude. An appreciation that had always been missing in her life.

She did not deserve him was her next consideration, but that one, too, disappeared into the following realisation. He had given her Alex's note unopened.

Tearing the paper apart she looked down at the words and saw a sheet of self-importance and weakness. Alex blamed her for all that had happened to him. He had been to see her mother and had laid all his arguments before her and was pleased to see that she agreed with him. He asked for her to meet him, at his house, at night where they might go on from where they had left off. He told her that no one truly understood him apart from her and that the world was a place that had been cruel to him and harsh. It was not his fault that things had turned out as they had, but his father's. There ought to have been better provision for his mother and for him—after all, how was a man to live and prosper on nothing? He said he had heard of the evil in Simeon Morgan. He finished by saying that she was his love and always would be, until the very end of time.

She ripped up the note after she had read it and placed all the pieces in her bin. The truth of Alexander Thompson rang out from every single written word. He was insubstantial, needy and narcissistic and was a man who would end up exactly like her mother. A bitter shell. A believer in nothing.

Simeon had been born into a family who had no time for him, yet he had forged ahead and succeeded, despite opposition, regardless of birth.

He had triumphed over adversity and without complaint. He had found a position in the world even though he had been born without one. He had not expected anyone else to provide for him.

Tears came to her eyes.

He was still doing it now. With her. With Flora and Catherine Rountree. With Athelridge Hall. With her mother and her sister.

With those poorer people who would benefit from the new rail connection to London. And those were the ones that she knew of.

Well, there was only one thing for it. She had to show him that she was worthy of him and to do that she needed to be here, in London, beside him. She could begin with Flora. She would begin with a child her own father had tried to kill. There was at least some justice in that.

Early in the afternoon she came across Flora Rountree in the garden to one side of the building. She was sitting on the ground picking buttercups and daisies, her scraggly posy reminding Adelia of her young years when she used to do exactly the same.

'Do you thread them sometimes into a necklace?' she asked softly, not wishing to startle the child.

'No.' Her little face was solemn as she sat up straight.

'Shall I show you, then?'

The slight nod was encouraging.

Finding her own long-stemmed daisies, Adelia pushed her thumb nail through the thick stem and threaded a new flower through. Then she did the same to the next flower and the next one after that. The ring of daisies began to grow.

'The small buttercups work, too, but you have to get the ones with the thickest stalks otherwise it is much more difficult.'

'You are very pretty, Mrs Morgan. Prettier than anyone I have ever seen. Prettier even than a princess.'

'Thank you, Flora.'

'My mama always said I was plain.' She did not look up as she said this, the posy in her hand twirling around and around.

'Well, beauty is something that is not always seen. Kindness is beautiful.'

'So is the truth.'

This was unexpected and Adelia waited, hoping for an explanation. A moment later she got it.

'Uncle Simeon tells the truth. He never lies. That is beautiful to me.'

'I like that, too.'

'He said I can stay here for ever with him, until I don't want to. He does not break his promises.'

'No, I don't think he does.'

'A man tried to kill me.'

This came from nowhere and Adelia felt her teeth clench together. A man. Her father.

'Mama stopped him, but he hit her, too. Now she is dead.'

Adelia sat on the lawn beside her. 'You are safe here, Flora. No one will ever hurt you again. I promise.'

'That's what Uncle Simeon said, too. He gave me this.' She pulled at a plaited leather strap around her neck and a small ceramic bird came into her hand. 'It was his when he was young and he told me that it helped.'

'Helped with what?'

'Dreams. He said you could fly off to the land of dreams with this around your neck and sleep well because of it.'

The poignancy of what was being said and what wasn't left a lump in Adelia's throat.

'Perhaps we could all go on a picnic together. Would you like that?'

A short nod followed, not as convincing as Adelia might have wanted, but it was at least a start.

'I will ask Uncle Simeon, then, and see if it is possible.'

The next nod was more solid, although when her governess came through to the garden,

Adelia knew that their chat was over. Watching the little girl disappear, she was surprised as her husband came out to join her.

'So that is a daisy chain...' he said and stopped.

'You have not made one before?'

'Meadows of flowers in bloom were few and far between in the back streets of Manchester.'

He looked away then, and Adelia sensed he would have liked to have said more, but he did not. The distance was back and the caution.

'I promised Flora a picnic as soon as we were able to organise it.'

'Where were you thinking of going?'

'Hyde Park, perhaps. Somewhere by the Serpentine might be nice and we could sail leaf boats.'

'Another of your childhood games?'

'Mama used to be less sad once and was a woman who enjoyed life.'

'And your father?'

'Was seldom there, so I hope you can come. Presenting a united front might be just the thing needed to pull Flora from her melancholy. She remembers my father trying to hurt her.'

'I know.'

'Are there other children around here that she might play with? Someone around her age?'

'I am not sure.'

'Perhaps we could ask my sister Charlotte to come to London, then. A holiday would do her good, I think.'

'The one who looks about as sad as Flora does?'

'Well, isn't it said that misery loves company?'

He laughed. 'If you think it a wise idea, I will send a message up with my driver asking if your sister can come here. A maid could be dispatched to go with them to bring her back to London.'

'I think she would like that.'

She saw a muscle throb in his cheek as he glanced up at the house, all the windows of the place overlooking the garden. Awareness rang between them, holding them still, but then he moved back and the spell was broken, a gardener turning the corner with a barrow even as he did so.

Had Simeon heard him coming, for he always seemed very aware of his surroundings? A vestige from his childhood, perhaps? She had been exactly the same around her father, never relaxing for a moment in his company lest he lash out in anger.

Simeon was large and well muscled and gave the impression that he could handle anyone or anything that might come at him. But that was now. She thought about the small child who might have known things very differently, a boy lost between adults with little honour until the old uncle with the kind face in the painting had come to save him.

No wonder he had empathy for Flora Rountree. No wonder he wanted to help her. Perhaps he saw a lot of himself in the young girl, scowling and untrusting, a boy from the hard streets of life with little to recommend it.

She made herself smile and gave him some advice. 'If you could find some time for the picnic, I am sure Flora would appreciate it.'

His nod was quick before he turned.

At least he was not yet leaving for the north and she was not being packed off to Athelridge Hall. The suggestion of bringing Charlotte down to London had merit, too. Her sister had had her struggles and perhaps a complete change of scenery might be good to pull her from her sadness. Adelia was certain she would be kind to Flora and that was another bonus, two young girls with their secrets and fears and the hope that maybe by sharing stories they could both begin to heal.

Charlotte arrived the next afternoon and for the first time in a long while Adelia saw excitement in her face.

'Mama did not much want me to come, Adelia, but I told her that I would run away if she did not allow it, run away and never come back and I meant it. Athelridge Hall is just so very tedious at the moment and Mama's sadness is like a blanket over everything.'

'Well, I hope you will enjoy it here. I have put you in the room next to mine if you are agreeable to that. Otherwise, if you prefer it, you can sleep in my room with me.'

'No, I would like a room of my own. Does it have a view?'

'It does. You can see the church spire and the outline of London's buildings across the trees. Tomorrow I was hoping we might have a picnic on the grass in the nearby park early in the afternoon. Mr Morgan has the care of a girl called Flora who needs cheering up as her mother has just died and we were hoping that you might be a friend to her, Charlotte.'

'Of course I shall. It is all so wonderful to be asked to London for a holiday. Will Mr Morgan mind me being here? He was not very happy at the wedding and I thought perhaps he did not like any of us. Mama has never forgiven him for the lack of a wedding breakfast and for leaving us at the chapel in Hyde Park without even a ride home. She speaks of it all the time.'

'Sometimes being an adult is difficult, Charlotte, and the wedding was stressful, but Mr Morgan and I have sorted things out between us now, so don't worry.'

'You being away from home has made me appreciate how much you do for us all, Adelia, and I don't think I ever thanked you for that. With Father and everything…you took a lot of his anger on yourself and it was unfair. Mother should have been stronger, I think, but she is just not.'

Adelia held out her arms and pulled Charlotte in for a hug. When her sister was younger they had been close so it was nice to feel that again.

'Life is what you make it and Mr Morgan is a good man despite what Mama says.'

That evening when both the girls were asleep Adelia went downstairs to see if she could find Simeon. He had asked her to come for a drink when she was less busy and she located him again in his library working diligently on some large plans spread out across his desk.

'Are the girls settled in?'

'They are. Flora asked if she might sleep in with Charlotte and my sister was most agreeable. It seems they will be friends.'

'A further triumph, then. You are very good at making the world right about you, Adelia.'

'I have had lots of practice and under difficult circumstances.' She looked at the plans, intricate angled drawings of cross sections and beams and fastenings. 'Are these for your new railway?'

'They are. I am looking at the gradients and trying to work out angles, though as I told you I need another challenge after all this. Something different.'

'Well, I am certain you will come up with one. Everyone at the Greys' dinner party who I talked with thought you were a genius.'

'Make enough money and people are bound to say that.'

'I don't think it was just the money, Simeon.'

He looked up when she used his name.

'I think it is more the fact that they can never quite work out who you are.'

'Are you suggesting my past might have been a help?'

'I am. No one truly knows you, knows what would pull you this way or that. It keeps them guessing.'

'My childhood was not a romantic one, Adelia.'

He'd only occasionally spoken of his past so she had no real idea of how bad it had been. But she did know he'd gained a strength from adversity and used it to his advantage.

'Neither was mine.'

That small honesty sat for a moment between them.

'Your sister looked happier than I remember her.'

'A result of our father's death, I should imagine. She no longer has to look over her shoulder and dread what is coming.'

'And you?'

'I don't, either. If I ever have children, I shall make sure that they are loved and valued and that no one will ever hurt them.'

The truth of what she'd just said suddenly dawned on her. Children were something they had never discussed and it was poor taste to have blurted that out given the state of their marriage.

He seemed to dismiss the implications completely, though, and continued on in a different vein altogether.

'I have made arrangements to go out to Richmond tomorrow and I wondered if you and the girls would like to accompany me? I will be leaving here around eleven. You had mentioned a picnic?'

Delight ran through her. 'Flora and Charlotte would love that. I know they would.'

'And you?' The question was softly given. 'Would you like that, too?'

She felt a blush rising and looked away. 'I've never been to Richmond before, but I hear it is very pretty.'

'I have someone designing a house for the land I've bought. He will be there at two on the site and I would appreciate your opinion on the place.'

He almost sounded as if he meant it and that this house might be important to them both in the future, a house that sat on the river among trees and birdsong.

'Will you move to Richmond after it is finished?'

'I think so. I want a change and that is just one part of it.'

'Will there be a garden there?' The house rose in her imagination, strong and beautiful.

'There will, but I don't want anything to be too formal.' He looked at her more closely. 'Why do you ask?'

'I have a vegetable patch at Athelridge, but lately I have been experimenting with flowers...'

Breaking off, she realised her mistake. No woman of means and good birth ever gardened and she had let a lot more slip than simply her love of the soil.

'You fed your family, didn't you? To make ends meet and in spite of your father?'

'Yes.'

'A fact that explains the trousers you were wearing on my first visit to Athelridge as well as the mud on your socks.'

'I wondered if you had seen that.'

'Is my bookkeeper giving you enough to live on?'

'More than enough.'

'Your father was a cheat, Adelia. He kept his

mistresses in style and yet allowed his family to nearly starve.'

She remained quiet.

'Athelridge Hall came to me through an investment scheme your father had gambled on that had turned bad. It was part of a portfolio that one of my investors had put up and I only remembered I had the papers when you visited that night.'

'Believe me, there were many other poor choices, too, because my father had no sense in business.'

'But his title helped?'

She nodded. 'I am glad it has gone to someone else. I am glad it is no longer here in my family, a ball and chain of expectation.'

He laughed then, loud and long.

'You are a constant surprise to me, Adelia. Sometimes I wonder if I know you at all.'

His gold eyes darkened and she sensed a change, no longer distant but much more aware.

'If you could alter one thing about yourself, what would it be?'

She didn't even need to think about it. 'I would like to laugh more. I would like to stop being scared.'

'Hell.'

Simeon swore a lot, but this time she only felt the warmth in the words as if he was angry with all the world, but not with her.

'Perhaps that can be arranged, this laughter. Outings with children invariably produce humour and we have two little girls who would suit our purpose admirably,' he said.

'Alexander Thompson was a friend I had growing up. He helped me learn things and manage the estate. I was thankful to him, but that was all.' The words were torn out of her, seemingly from nowhere, as though desperate to be uttered.

He looked startled. 'You don't have to explain your past to me, Adelia. It's what happens from now on that counts.'

'I thought I loved him once.' She gave the words with honesty, wanting Simeon to hear them.

'And now?' he asked, as though he couldn't help himself.

'Now I know that I don't.'

His smile caught her out, so honest and true. She wanted to tell him more. She wanted to say that the way she knew such a thing was because of him. Once love struck it had made every other emotion in life seem diluted. But she could not say that to him yet.

'While we are confessing our pasts I should tell you before anyone else does that I was married before, at nineteen, to a woman I thought I loved.'

'What happened?' Adelia decided in that moment not to mention that he'd already told her the bare bones of this when he'd been drunk on their wedding night. She was too curious to know more.

'She died eleven months after we married and then I concentrated on business.'

'And made an outrageous fortune?'

He laughed again. 'At twenty-seven the scars of life seem less painful somehow than they did at nineteen. After a distance of several years there must be a softening, for I was a lot angrier back then.'

'At this wife?'

'No, not at her because we never loved each other as we should have. More at the injustices of life, at the unfairness of being vulnerable.'

'And you were that? Vulnerable?'

'Once.'

He did not touch her, but she felt the heat

of him, the sense of him close and the knowing of him in some way that defied logic. She understood what he said instinctively because she had felt this vulnerability, too, tossed into a family that was weak in every part that mattered and having to find a way to save it.

And here she was on the other side of all of that, in a place of security and safety, a place where she no longer had to struggle and fight and worry. And it was all because of him.

'I said when I met you that I would offer you anything you wanted of me in our marriage and I meant it. You have, after all, kept your side of the bargain and I mean to keep to my own.'

She saw how he swallowed and how his glance fell across her body, in a manner that told her he had understood her meaning exactly.

'I should not want only duty from you, Adelia. There are other avenues...'

'Of course.'

The bubble broke. He was speaking of his mistress, the beautiful woman at their wedding, sultry and sensual, who would give him more than she ever could with her innocence and her uncertainty.

* * *

She was back to being prickly and after such an offer his good will was being sorely tested. For heaven's sake! What did she want from him? Had she just offered him her body or was he completely mistaken?

His own libido leapt to attention and he was glad that he sat behind a desk. That could not have been her message, a daughter of breeding and blood lines reaching back across the ages.

It was his own needs reacting, erroneously, incorrectly, in desperation and in hopefulness. He needed to get a grip on himself before he ruined everything, needed to get back to the innocuous picnic plans and the subject of the girls.

'I will instruct the staff to pack food baskets for the morrow. I think the day will be a warm one, but there is a cold wind blowing so we will take blankets.'

Simeon could barely believe the stream of words coming from his mouth—mild, bland, inoffensive nothings that cancelled out her offer and left him stranded still, on a shore he had not ventured to much before. The shore of folly and inanity and irresolution.

How did she do this so easily? To him? How

did she turn his mind to things she could not possibly have meant, crude things, things she would certainly not welcome from him? He needed to be a gentleman, he needed to make her feel safe. The sensations rushing around his body were not anything like that. No, they were conducive only to chaos.

'That will be lovely.'

Her words made him frown. What? he thought. What will be lovely? What on earth had they just spoken of? He was all at sea and struggling for comprehension. The idea of her beneath him right there on the carpet with the light of the chandelier on her body and the door locked was paramount in his mind. He imagined her hair down, all the glorious vibrant colours of it flowing through his fingers. He imagined his hands grasping her softness. And his tongue... Swallowing hard, he tried desperately to take stock of what she was saying to him.

'Goodnight. I hope you sleep well.'

More of her words. Then she was gone, walking out with a quiet grace, a woman who was refined and polished and poised.

All the things that he had tried to be, but was not. He wanted to follow her and ask her exactly what she had meant by her promise to allow him anything, to clarify her meaning, to know she was only speaking in general terms, to fully comprehend that she had not even remotely intended to ask him to make love to her. If he wanted to.

And he did want to.

So desperately his whole body had hardened. He quivered like some sort of a musical string wound as tightly as the tension would allow. He could barely believe the thickness of his desire.

Lust ruled him, simply and crudely, reminding him of the men in his childhood who had let it rule them. Such a thought sickened him, nauseated him, abruptly making him feel repulsive and shocked.

He had tried for so long to be rid of his past, been so careful to make sure that the messages he received from women were exactly as they had meant them. But he could not read his wife at all.

He closed his eyes and ran one hand through his hair, bringing himself back, finding a reassurance in his returning calm.

The sheets of paper with all the calculations

were comforting, too. His world was one of commerce and management.

He remembered his first years studying engineering and mathematics as an apprentice in his Uncle Jamie's workshops. The world of absolutes, the place of exactness where there was no room for even the slightest deviation or mistake.

It was like finding out the truth and returning to a welcomed tranquillity after all the turbulence of his childhood. He loved the control, he welcomed the rules and the constraint and the restrictions. He knew what was expected of him there and he relished the lack of surprises.

Yet now here he was, pounced on from all sides by uncertainty, stalked by disarray and confusion. And confronted at every turn by a woman who was beyond beautiful and yet did not truly know it.

A change. In everything.

He smiled then, because he'd wanted a variance, a difference in his life and he had got the biggest one he could have ever imagined.

Adelia Hermione Josephine Bennett Worthington had walked into his life. An angel, a devil, a saviour, a temptation. He wondered for a moment if he was going mad, if the stress of the past few months had finally got to him and addled his mind.

He thought of his uncle and his words of encouragement, the kindness he had shown and the guidance. Without Jamie he would never have survived. He would never have had the chance to. He turned to the picture behind him and took in the portrait, thanking the man as he had a thousand times before across the years. Missing him, but feeling the sadness and savouring it.

Tomorrow they would all go on a picnic to Richmond, to the river and the trees and the sunshine. He would see the children laugh and he would look at Adelia and be only thankful, all the darker thoughts gone, disappeared into the daylight. He would show her the drawings of the house and the fall of the land. They might make daisy chains or sail leaf boats and the food would be delicious and bountiful.

A proper day. A suitable outing.

He remembered his uncle finding him finally at fourteen in Angel Meadow, after months of searching for the lost child of his niece. Jamie had simply taken him home to his substantial house in the north of Manchester and showed him a life that he had no notion of.

A gentle life with enough to eat and any danger held at arm's length. His uncle had never been married and they had become family to each other, his quiet teachings helping Simeon to make sense of what had happened to him and to want a new beginning.

He was different now and better because of Jamie's kindness and integrity. There was no longer hatred in his heart. Adelia would see only the man he had invented, the man his uncle had fostered, the man the world had allowed to be reborn, one with luck on his side and strength in his vision.

Simeon liked this version of himself, but in order to keep it intact he would need to be very careful around his most singular wife.

Adelia had never seen such a beautiful place. The land that would hold the house her husband had drawn up was a large elevated slice of trees, grass and wild flowers, the Thames River lapping at its feet. The wind was quieter here, blocked off by a hill a few hundred yards away and the sunlight spilled down over it, warming both the earth and her heart.

Flora and Charlotte were chasing each other around the boughs of substantial oaks and elms. Everywhere there was peace and light, the loop of the river wide here and the water slow.

She loved Athelridge Hall, but this place was even more beautiful. History clothed the surrounds and a sense of the future here rather than the past made her stop and just enjoy the moment. She wanted to know this place with all of her heart.

Simeon had been distant this morning. Oh, granted he had been unfailingly polite and courteous to them all, but he was holding something back, the man she had spoken with last night now far more formal and stiff. His meeting with the architect had been a quick one and as she walked across to him after the man left she saw how carefully he watched the girls.

'They are happy here, Simeon. It is a good place. I can see why anyone would buy this piece of land. It's only a wonder the vendor sold it.'

He smiled, the first real humour she had seen all morning. 'Elijah Greene was an old man and the house he had built here burned down in a fire ten years ago. When I told him I was interested in buying the property he asked me many questions until he was satisfied I would be the right one.'

'Questions?'

'He wanted a house on it that would sit on the land with ease. He wanted a family here, too.'

'But you did not have one?'

'Strange, then, how things work out. He would have loved seeing the children running around the trees he had planted all those years ago.'

'A sense of history?'

'Exactly.'

He turned then to look at the river again, its surface glinting grey green in the light.

'Elijah asked if I might fashion a loggia under that elm by the river as a place of memory for him and I agreed. See the large piece of stone in the shadows? The loggia will sit there, its floor above the water so the sounds of the Thames can be heard.'

'That was an unusual request.'

'He was born here. It seemed fitting somehow to do as he asked.'

'A sense of place, you mean?'

'And one I never had myself.'

It was the most personal thing he had ever

said to her and after the distance he'd put between them that day she was surprised.

'We will start the construction of it in the next few weeks. The house will be built of cream stone and will be long and low. A solid house that will last for a thousand years and beyond. Safe and constant.'

'A fortress like the Tower of London?' She smiled as she said it.

'No,' he returned, 'only a home.'

Flora had come to them now, her hands full of cornflowers, buttercups and daisies.

'There are so many flowers here. I am going to pick some and bring them back to London. Charlotte is finding a bunch, too.'

Adelia bent down to smell them, the buttercup grazing her chin, and Flora smiled as she wiped the pollen away. It was so good to see Catherine Rountree's child happy, her cheeks flushed and her hands full of flowers.

'Put them on the blanket here in the shade, Flora, and go and tell Charlotte that I am about to lay out the food for afternoon tea.'

Adelia was pleased that no maid or governess accompanied them today, the freedom of being here like this undeniably relaxing. The driver and footman were with the carriage by the roadside, tending to the horses and having a rest themselves.

Leaning down, she plucked a blue cornflower from the bunch and handed it to Simeon.

'For friendship,' she said, 'and for fortune and prosperity. An apt plant for today, I think.'

He took it and tucked it into a buttonhole on his jacket so that the spindly stem showed underneath and she laughed, because with the sun on his dark hair and a flower above his heart Simeon was the most beautiful man she had ever seen.

'There is a language around flowers?' His question was puzzled.

'There is and it is extensive and symbolic.' She plucked a buttercup from Flora's posy. 'This represents humility and neatness. And a daisy is new beginnings.'

She did not add fertility or love because those words seemed out of place here today and she needed to understand just what he wanted of her first.

'You are a mine of information, Lia.'

The nickname he had used at the ball. She looked up and caught him watching her, but his eyes slid away as soon as she did so.

Not so much distant, then, but cautious. She

was glad for it. She would need to leave it to him to make the first move towards any intimacy if that was what he wanted, for her words yesterday had clearly left him tense.

A poor way to begin a picnic, but she had never been one to simply give up and so she found good humour and tried to act as if all the world was still only wonderful.

Chapter Ten

He needed to relax and he knew it. Adelia looked as though he had sliced all her dreams of this day into pieces and was now trying in her own particular way to glue them back together again so that none of the rough edges showed. He liked that about her. He imagined she had done the same all her life for a family ruled by a destructive man and wished she did not feel the need to do so here with him.

The blue flower in his lapel was beautiful and the sun had come out now, fully sending the land into bright swathes and darker shadows. It reminded him of a painting his uncle had had in the house he had first been brought to, a dirty, thin and afraid youth who was astonished by the number of books just lying around and by furnishings in large rooms that were not ragged or worn.

He banished the image and sought for happier things. Flora was laughing as she dashed towards them, Adelia's sister Charlotte behind her with another larger bunch of wildflowers.

They arrived beside him like two rambunctious puppies, each with their own story to tell about the land and the water and the fun they were having. All of the things he had imagined once when Elijah Greene had sold him this land, all the things he had promised himself he would have.

Why wasn't he happier, then?

He looked across at his wife, his own unease translated to her, and knew the answer.

He wanted her body, but he wanted her mind, too. He wanted her love and her loyalty and all the years of a good life together. He wanted someone he could depend on and trust and talk to and be with. He didn't want a half-promise or a weakened troth. He didn't want a marriage of convenience either, flung together by circumstance, fused by necessity or force.

Flora brought him over a plate, and he sat on the edge of the blanket and looked down at the food.

'I swear Mrs Williams is the finest pastry cook I have had.'

'Her biscuits and cake are good, too,' Flora

said, wiping the crumbs of gingerbread from her chin. 'Mama always told me that when she was little she never had enough to eat and you didn't either, Uncle Simeon.'

Simeon smiled. She had stopped calling him Mr Morgan and had begun to use his given name and he liked it.

'Mama told me that you used to go and steal food and that you got caught sometimes and then she didn't see you for a few weeks at a time. She said you were her hero, is that true?'

Both Adelia and Charlotte seemed to be waiting for an answer from him.

'I could run fast, but sometimes not fast enough.'

The girls both laughed, but Adelia didn't, her eyes filling with worry and comprehension.

She'd seen the scar on his hand, but she hadn't glimpsed the ones on his back. Stealing had held stiff penalties on the dangerous streets of Rochdale Road and Gould Street in Angel Meadow. He remembered being left after one beating in the burial ground of St Michael's Church, thousands of bones of paupers unburied all around him, like luminescent ghosts in the moonlight.

He looked towards the river, trying to re-group. Why were these memories flooding back with so much more fervour? Why could he no longer push them down and away as he had always done, a layer of forgetfulness buffering any recollection between then and now?

He knew the answer to that question even as he asked it. It was all because of Adelia. She had uncovered the hope in his life that he had long since lost. Possibility shimmered now as it never had before and a future he had thought unattainable had suddenly become a prospect.

A joyful heart is good medicine, but a crushed spirit dries up the bones.

He'd read this once in the Bible at his uncle's house shortly after he'd been brought there and the small verse had echoed inside him down through the years.

Was it possible to cure his spirit with a joyful heart? If bits of you were lost, could other parts replace them? Could healing come from trust and belief?

Biting into the lamb pie, Simeon tasted mint and other flavourings. He washed the mouthful down with a bottle of cider, still cold from being on ice at his town house.

He needed to try.

'Would you take a walk with me, Adelia, to the river after this? I have something to speak to you about.'

'Of course. The girls can make daisy chains while we are gone and I shall award prizes for the best endeavour.'

Charlotte and Flora both laughed and gulped down their pie and cake and within a few moments he was walking with his wife along the river path.

When he failed to speak she picked up small, flat stones and hurled them into the water, counting the skips out loud. She knew he wanted to say something, so she allowed him the time and space he needed, then finally he did.

'I am not quite as you imagine me, Adelia.' He stopped and swallowed before carrying on. 'I am…damaged.'

'How?'

'You had one father who was a violent man and you suffered, but… I had many…fathers… who were both violent and evil. I lost any innocence I had before I was eight and continued to do so until my great-uncle came to find me when I was fourteen and took me away.'

'From Manchester?'

'From Angel Meadow. A place of residence for the destitute Irish and those who had no time for any sort of law and order. Stealing food was the smallest of the sins I have committed, some for a good cause and some...not. I told you once that I only bed courtesans and mistresses, but I was not entirely honest with you as to the reason why.'

'The why?' He was shaking now. She saw how he threaded his hands together and deposited them behind his back.

'I killed a man. It was after my stepbrother had died. I had no money to pay for Geordie's funeral, you see, and I thought I could earn it with my body in the street where prostitution occurred, but when it came down to a willing act, I found I could not. As I ran to get away the man attacked me and I got hold of a piece of wood on the side of the road and whacked him back...'

He stopped.

'I will not lie to you, I would do it again in self-defence, but the person I have become is not the one that I was once and I thought you should understand that because...because I want us to know each other better.'

'I would like that, too.' Her own voice wavered, not in doubt, but in sorrow for the boy he had had to be to survive, for the child inside him that had never had a chance.

Those in society spoke of his childhood as if it was a romantic one, as if it had been the making of him, as if in all the adventures and excitement a man had been formed in the shape of one who could take on the world and had done so, when the very opposite was true.

Simeon Morgan's childhood had destroyed him, utterly, in spirit and in flesh. It had taken away hope and trust and belief and here he was trying to rebuild again, rebuild a dream, just like the house he'd described on the land on which they stood. Solid and safe and constant.

He was the bravest man she had ever met.

He stepped forward and took her hand, one finger brushing across the gold of her wedding ring.

'This was my uncle's mother's ring. Her name was Eleanor Morgan and she was from a good family. James Morgan gave it to me on the morning of the day that he died.'

Tears formed in her eyes and fell down her cheeks, the ring taking on an importance that it had not had before. She found it hard to speak.

'Thank you for telling me that.'

Without replying, he kissed her hand, like a knight of old, a warrior who had won the war, but not his own battles, but, at this moment in the sun by the river in Richmond it was enough. Enough to begin with and build on, enough to risk everything.

'We started this marriage with conflict and discord, but perhaps if we are honest with each other we could find something finer between us. I hope that can be the case, Adelia. A new beginning. From now. I promise that I won't rush you.'

She wanted to say he should, that rushing was exactly what she did want, but sense stopped her for the truths he had just told her were hard ones. Now she needed to earn his trust again so that the deceit she had used in forcing this marriage was softened and forgotten.

'A new beginning sounds like a good plan, Simeon.' She put her hand out, and he shook it. 'Let there be only honesty in our marriage from now.'

He smiled. 'Only that.'

* * *

Simeon sat beside her on the carriage ride back to London with the girls opposite and she could feel his thigh against her own.

Flora and Charlotte were thrilled with their day and had decided this was what they would like to do each week, come to Richmond with a picnic and find flowers.

'Every season will be different,' Charlotte said. 'We can find snowdrops in winter and daffodils in the spring. Would those flowers grow there, Adelia?'

'I am certain they would, Charlotte.' But her attention was not really on flowers. It was on her husband at her side, his hand on his lap, his wide gold wedding ring encircling his fourth finger. She wanted to place her own hand on top of his, for she had never known this tingle of excitement before, as if every second was special and wanton.

Flora had taken up the conversation now. 'You asked me once to think about what I wanted to do, Uncle Simeon, and now I know. I want to have a garden, like Adelia does at Athelridge. Charlotte told me of it.'

'Well, there's certainly enough room out at Richmond for a substantial plot.'

'See, Charlotte, I said to you that he would be happy with that. We can choose seeds together and plant them, anything we like and anything that grows. We can sell them when they flower to the houses around here, for they certainly look rich.'

As she laughed at the children's plans Adelia caught her husband's eyes and saw how he watched her. Everyone all her life had told her how beautiful she was and until now she had never truly believed it, but here in this conveyance she finally did. Beauty was not attached so much to the outside but to the inside and her insides were full of joy and delight and anticipation.

This trip was endless, Simeon thought. He couldn't believe he had told her of his past in such a raw and brutal way, for he'd never before said a word of it to anyone save to his uncle in those first few months of being saved. The confession had both exhausted and freed him, which was a strange thing to think, exhausted him with the memory and freed him because Adelia had understood his pain and had responded to it.

Today had been astounding, his land beneath their feet and the girls frolicking with laughter and flowers.

But it was Adelia who had restored his hope with her acceptance of who he was and who he had been. She had not closed up, she had struggled with what he had told her, he knew that, but it was because she was sad for him and not disgusted for herself. Then when he had said he wanted more in this marriage, she had stood there and stated that she did, too. No games played, no coquetry, no pretence in it, but an honesty and generosity of spirit.

He'd wanted to kiss her and hold her close, but he'd also promised that he would not rush her. Turning to watch the countryside through the window, he frowned.

He'd told Adelia some things from his past, but by no means had he said it all. Still, she had not run for all she was worth, she was still sitting here next to him, the warmth of the line of one shapely thigh running down the length of his own. He concentrated on the connection and relaxed. There was plenty of time.

He wondered what the night would bring after the children were put to bed. He wanted to sit and talk with Adelia and kiss her again. Just the vision of it had him worked up and he shook such rumination away. This was neither the time nor the place for those thoughts and he was glad when finally his town house came into view.

Flora's governess greeted them at the front door, shepherding the two children off and leaving him and Adelia alone.

'I need a drink. Would you like to join me?' The confines of the ride had made him jittery.

He used the small sitting room this time as his place of choice. It had always been one of his favourite rooms in the house as the garden seemed closest here and, even in September, it was still in full show. He saw his wife take in the riot of autumn colour and smile.

'It was one of the reasons I bought this place,' he said as he poured them each a white wine.

'The decorating is more simple in here than the other downstairs rooms, isn't it?'

'That is because I chose what I liked.'

'Who did the rest, then?'

'Mr Mullins, one of the most sought-after decorators in London at the moment. He came highly recommended, though I thought his taste too busy in all honesty and wanted it more restful in here.'

'I see.' He liked the way she smiled for it lit up the green in her eyes. Her glance went then to the shelf of books sitting at one end of the room, clearly a selection of old favourites, and she wandered over to take a look.

'You enjoy the history of Ancient Rome?'

'I do. Any civilisation that can shift from a monarchy to a republic and maintain an immense empire for twelve centuries is to be applauded.'

'I have heard it said that if you cannot understand history you may not understand yourself.'

He liked the way she stood after giving him this statement as if waiting for an answer.

'An acknowledgement of the past, you mean?'

'Embracing and accepting it, I suppose, all the pieces making sense of who you are now.'

'And just who are we now, Adelia?' He'd had enough of the oblique talk and wanted some direct answers. He could see the shock in her eyes, but carried on anyway. 'Who are we exactly to each other?'

She took a while to answer, but he waited.

'Friends, perhaps?' she offered hesitantly.

'I want more.'

He put his cards straight down on the table, like a business proposition, though the fright in her eyes was noticeable.

What exactly was he saying? Adelia wondered as the moments stretched out in silence. She was unsure of what it was he sought. She could hear the voice of a businessman in all the words, the options, the contingencies, the conditions. He did not even look particularly happy when he said it and this confused her further.

A knock on the door had them both turning and Harris gave the message that a constable, Mr McInnes, was outside waiting to see Simeon.

'Send him in.'

Her husband looked over at her with something akin to frustration. 'He won't be staying long,' he promised her.

Then the man was there, hat in hand.

'There has been an accident, Mr Morgan. Tom Brady is in hospital after being set upon by ruffians and he is calling for you.'

'Is it...?' Simeon didn't finish the words, but both she and Mr McInnes knew exactly what he meant.

'He has lost a lot of blood.'

Already Simeon was following him out.

'I am sorry, Adelia, we will have to talk again tomorrow. This is important.'

'Of course.' She remembered the tall man who had smiled at her during her wedding even as her husband had left without a backward glance.

To keep herself busy when he had gone, Adelia decided to look through the bookshelf, for he'd said she was most welcome to borrow anything she wanted to.

Apart from the many books on Ancient Rome there were other novels and short stories, some of which she had read and others she hadn't. A thin volume in red velvet caught her attention on the bottom shelf and she pulled it out, seeing immediately on opening it that it was a book of handwritten poems.

Not just any poems, either, but bawdy ones speaking of things that a man might do to a woman in bed.

Turning to the front of the book, she almost dropped it. The small journal was dedicated to Simeon and it was from Theodora Wainwright, the red-headed woman at their wedding and his mistress.

The poems were extremely lewd and not very well written, but after a few moments she realised there were other things at play here and she should not be prying into something so private. Theodora Wainwright had clearly loved Simeon with all her heart, but many words echoed her thoughts of his continued distance and his reserve.

Snapping the book shut, Adelia replaced it, making sure that it lined up exactly with the other books around it. Then she took a novel she had not read from the very top shelf and let herself out of the sitting room. She knew Simeon would not have wanted her to find that journal and wondered at his own reaction to the book. Had Theodora Wainwright given it to him in the early days of their relationship or was it a more recent gift?

There were so many pieces of her husband that she had no knowledge of, disparate facts and unfamiliar people, like a jigsaw puzzle where, because of the gaps and missing fragments, the whole was hard to understand.

That night she waited up for Simeon and when she heard footsteps in the corridor she gave him some time before she ventured out of her room.

His room was quiet, but she knew he was there because in the crack of light under the door she saw a shadow. She did not knock, but turned the handle carefully and simply walked in.

He was faced away from her and shirtless, but instead of smooth brown skin on his back there was a criss-crossing of old scarring, a shocking travesty that left her breathless and still. She hardly dared to move, but he had seen her already, turning and dragging the shirt off the bed next to him across his shoulders and on in one smooth motion.

Huge and dark and half-dressed, the scowl across his face was fully formed and unhidden. His hair was loose and there were bruises on the knuckles of both his hands.

'I am sorry—'

She broke off even as he shook his head.

'Don't be.'

He thought she spoke of his scars?

'No, I did not mean—'

But again he failed to let her finish.

'Tom Brady is recovering. He was set on by a group of youths and almost kicked to death.'

'Did the police find these people?'

'No. But after the constabulary failed to find them, Tom sent for me and told me who they were. Once I knew that, it was easy to locate them.'

'Because you hold ties with people like this and you know the places they would frequent?' She could not understand quite what it was that he said.

'Partly. Some people I knew back in Angel Meadow have moved down to the city and I see them sometimes, have a drink and find out how they are. They helped me track down the group that attacked Tom.'

Adelia could not believe he would tell her these things as if it were a normal occurrence, as if anyone would do the same for a friend who had suffered as Tom Brady had.

'Are the youths...still alive?'

He laughed at that. 'If I'd killed them, I would hardly be here.'

'You've hurt your hands?'

'A small inconvenience. Their heads were damn hard.'

'And ripped your shirt?'

She had begun to shake because it was all so horrible, so dangerous, so very foreign.

'You could have been killed, Simeon!'

He looked at her then in the way of someone who failed to fathom what she was saying. 'They got nowhere near me, Adelia.'

'How many of them were there?'

'Four. Well, six if you count the scrawny couple of hangers-on, which I didn't.'

Her hands came across her mouth in dismay. He was no longer the businessman who had fitted into society with such ease at the Greys' dinner party. No, this man in front of her now was far more dangerous and unknown. A man of blood and violence and retribution.

As if finally realising the depth of her distress, he breathed out hard.

'I told you I was damaged, Adelia, damaged well and truly, though God knows I have tried to make you feel safe both here and at Athelridge. But there are things you don't know about me and if you are unable...'

'I know that I don't want you dead.'

'I won't be.' His strangled words sounded as if he was trying to stop himself from laughing. 'I won't be.' He repeated this after a few seconds and now there was a sincerity in his tone that made her happier. 'I promise.'

At that she undid the buttons on her thick

cotton dressing gown and let it slip to the floor. It fell in a whoosh, the noise loud in a room of silence, leaving only the lace-edged night-dress beneath it.

'Nothing you could do would make me want to leave you, Simeon, and it is time that you knew it.'

'Well, it should.' He sounded stunned.

She moved then, towards him, towards his warmth and his strength and his damage until she was right next to him, an inch away.

'Existing across two worlds must sometimes be…hard.' She whispered this into his skin and saw his flesh rise into goose pimples.

'It would be harder without you.'

When his fingers threaded through her hair, she saw the bruising on his right hand was deep, the injuries substantial on each knuckle. She imagined the hatred and the danger that he must have been a part of.

'Is it finished? This revenge?'

'It is.'

He tipped her chin up so that she looked straight at him.

'But when I see something that is unjust or plain wrong I will act, Adelia. It is who I am.'

'I know that, too.'

She reached up and her arms knotted around his shoulders. She felt the scars on his back as her fingers opened to hold on. More violence and brutality, the cruelty written like a story.

And then he was lifting her into his arms and across to his high four-poster bed. His other hand pulled down the covers and he sat on the mattress carefully with her on his knee.

'I imagined this all the way back from Richmond in the carriage. You, here with me and undressed.'

'And I thought you were busy keeping your distance.'

'Only because I was afraid if I touched you I might never be able to let go.'

She was the most beautiful woman he had ever seen, every part of her, every inch he could see through the sheerness of fabric. Her skin was ivory and unmarked and so pale the blue bloodlines beneath were easily visible. Her hair lay about her in a curling mass, all the shades of blond and honey and white. Lifting a long curl, he laid it across his arm, dark against light, fragile against well worn, the scars on his forearm snaking up beneath, a further sign of who he was and all that she was not.

'I read some poems today in a book from the bottom shelf in your sitting room. They were written by your mistress.'

Lord! Theodora's journal, the one she had given him the last time they met.

'They talk of your emotional distance, Simeon. Theodora Wainwright never thought you were hers.'

'A wise deduction, then, because I wasn't.'

'Are you mine, then?'

'Yes.' He wanted her to stop talking. He wanted to shut the world out, banish all those who might take up their thoughts. He did not want to think of Theodora at all.

'I do not know the things she spoke of or the ways she describes the movements to make love…'

He kissed her to stop all the words, to find the silence, but she moved away and carried on.

'I don't want us to be like those poems.'

'We won't be, sweetheart,' he returned and tried not to smile. She looked so earnest and young and the one poem of Theodora's that he had browsed through before he had thrown the journal into the bottom of his bookcase unread was bordering on the absurdly erotic.

'I have seen animals on the farm so I do know some things…'

He turned her towards him on his lap and kept her still. He had not removed his trousers because he did not want to frighten her, but he knew she could feel him there, hard edged and ready. His whole body pulsed with need.

'Stop thinking, Lia, and just feel.'

The emerald green in her eyes was wide and fearful.

The truth exploded around him. Despite all she had said, he finally understood that she had not done this before. She was a virgin and he was rushing her and treating her as he did every other woman he had bedded—women of experience.

Pulling her into him, he sat there trying, in the moment, to find some sort of method to carry on and to make sense of things.

Then he had it.

Heaping the pillows up against the top bedstead, he brought her up to lie beside him, drawing small circles on the flesh at the top of her arm as he began to talk.

'My mother made creams for the skin of fine

ladies and I took it around Kensington with a pack of lies and a lot of bravado. It smelled nice, so it was not too hard to sell, but...'

He stopped and he saw that she was listening.

'But being in the vicinity of those houses and those people made me understand that there was another way of life, a life that was different from what I was used to. When I had sold out or nearly sold out of the cream I would often sit against the railings of the parks that abounded in the fancy squares and allowed myself to simply be. It was quiet and clean there and the people passing by seemed kind. I liked what they had and who they were even if to them I was probably a ragged beggar boy whom they would rather have had gone. But I watched them and I learnt and when I was finally rescued I became like them.'

'But not entirely?' Her query was soft.

'Who you were once never quite leaves you. It crouches there, waiting.'

At this, she reached out and took his hand in her own, turning over the palm so his swollen knuckles were on show.

'You try to make a difference in the world? To help people?'

She kissed his fingers one by one.

'I never visited Theodora again after our wedding, Adelia. I swear to God that I didn't.'

He felt her smile.

'Her poems were dreadful. I only read one. I didn't want to take the book in the first place, but she was insistent.'

'I found them...interesting.'

He felt a charge of hope run up his body. 'In what way?'

'Sometimes I feel I am...too...scared.' She had trouble finding her words. 'It's because of my father, I think. I always had to be careful and watching. I'd like to be braver.'

He sat up a bit more. Here was the opening he had been looking for.

'Close your eyes, then. Just for a moment.'

She did as he asked though there was a slight frown on her brow as he ran his finger across her cheek and around one ear.

'No, keep your eyes closed.'

This time, he circled her breast with one hand and he felt the small gasp of response.

'Don't move. Stay still. Just feel.'

His tongue laved her nipple through the lawn, soft at first and then with more force, the feel of it creating a rhythmical pulse that began to match the beat of her heart.

When her body rose of its own accord, he knew that he was winning. But still he went gently, lifting his head to place a line of kisses across her shoulder and throat.

She was smooth and lean, save for the swell of her breasts and the curve of her bottom. She looked as though the sun had not touched her anywhere. He imagined her out in her garden wreathed in fabric from head to toe and could not remember ever seeing skin like it. A siren bathed in the milk of moonlight.

He felt her fingers threading through his hair, pulling him up, and he went willingly and found her lips, his hand on her nape now and angling the kiss. When she opened her mouth he came in, deeper, tasting the sweetness of her, knowing the intimacy.

This was what a kiss should be like, Adelia thought, nothing between them but desire. She felt his strength and care and excitement burned through her.

His eyes watched her close, the gold burnished by need, nothing hidden.

'Love me, Simeon,' she barely whispered.

'I will,' he returned and a languid want made her world tip, into him, his scent, his touch, his honesty. There was so little left of only her.

His hand cupped her jaw and then fell lower, to slide the straps of her nightdress off her shoulder. Then he sat her up and the sheer lawn fell to her waist.

'God.' His voice sounded broken. 'You are so very beautiful, Adelia.'

She smiled because it was not her face that his eyes fastened upon, but her breasts, and that seemed right somehow, a beauty kept only for him and no one else.

'So unblemished,' he carried on, 'like alabaster.'

He stood now beside the bed and she watched him remove his trousers, the dark hair on his body mirrored in that around his groin, his masculinity standing proud.

He did not flinch as she looked and became accustomed to what she saw. His man's body, ready for her. She'd seen statues of the male physique in books hewn of cold marble, but this one was flesh and blood and warm and living.

'I won't hurt you, sweetheart. We can stop whenever...'

She reached out and touched him, the firm length of his sex in her hand and the magic of the sensual filling her. Just them. Just here. Just now. The secrets of their bodies in the night.

And he moved, too, to lie beside her, his hand on her stomach, gentle, soft, and then travelling down.

'Let me in, Lia. Let me know you.'

Closing her eyes, she felt her hips rising as he dwelt lower, his finger in her wetness, and pushing, inside, finding the centre of her joy.

Her flesh clenched around him, the truth of what he was doing dismantling any fear. All she wanted was for him to keep going as the waves began to build. His mouth was at one breast, now suckling in the same rhythm, and she moved with him, searching for the promise and then finding it as she tipped and fell headlong into the burning fire.

She heard herself groan and she felt his finger there inside her held by things she had no knowledge of, pulling him in further, never letting go.

Her whole body jolted time and time again, until, finally spent, she relaxed into the understanding of what had just happened.

* * *

He swore as if from a distance as she tried to find reality, her hand reaching for her gold cross as a touchstone.

'I never knew...' she tried to say and stopped.

'Neither did I,' he replied and rolled on top of her, opening her thighs and resting there, waiting till she looked at him, asking for permission.

He could not hold back. She was wet and hot and ready, her orgasm surprising him with its intensity and its suddenness. What would happen next?

When she nodded, he began to move, starting to push in and watching her carefully, her head tipped back, her thighs closing on him.

'No, sweetheart. Trust me.'

He did not want to hurt her, so he waited, the green of her glance taking in his words and need and then changing from brittle emerald to acquiescence.

'Now.' He said the word on a breath and slid further into her, the tightness exhilarating and foreign. A virgin. Pure. Untouched. Innocent.

His own sullied past should have stopped him, should have made him think twice, but it didn't. He was fire and flame and energy and she was kindling ready to be burned. He pushed in deep and then deeper, felt a tear and a release, her maidenhood plundered under his sex. When she cried out he stopped, but did not withdraw. He let her accustom herself to what he offered. Let her flesh expand around him and understand what its true purpose was.

Her eyes watched him, hooded and languid, like an unpractised siren poised on the edge of change, and then he moved. Only a little. A question. A permission. A sanction for more.

The pain of ecstasy, thin bound between them, bloomed. He felt it in a throb and heard it in her sigh, the rush of blood and the knowledge of more, only them in the darkness joined by life.

He came inside her fully, embedded in the final fusion. Her mouth opened, but the words did not come, her breath stilled by expectation. With intent he withdrew and came in again, harder this time and solid, the movement repeated even as she cried out and her nails seared down his back to keep him there, cleaved together, unbreakable. A shared passion, a communication of the flesh, their bodies moving in union onwards and upwards as a dance of release.

And it came, with a sureness and a potency, a concentration of feeling diluted only by delight.

Afterwards he lay there, fighting for his own breath, feeling the beat of his heart like a drum in his ears, echoing, calling.

Like dying. Fluid. Formless. Hardly moving.

He was a man who had spent all his years bedding experienced women he'd thought would fulfil his needs and here he was with his virgin wife, being driven beyond anything he had ever known before. It astounded him.

She was like quicksilver, volatile and unpredictable, with an edge of sweet innocence that charmed and delighted him.

When his breathing returned to normal he rolled on to his back and looked at the ceiling, the cool air of night-time welcomed.

'Thank you, Adelia.' He turned his head to see her smile. 'You were extraordinary.'

'Were?' Her voice held humour.

'Are,' he amended and sought for her hand, entwining his fingers with her own, feeling the connection between them. He had never held hands with a woman in bed before and the simple joy of it filled him up.

'I think you were better than any of those poems I looked at in the red-velvet book, Simeon,' she teased.

'I hope I didn't hurt you?'

'For a second you did and then all I could feel was the promise.'

'A promise that is a slippery slope, my beautiful wife.'

'Why?'

'Because with lots of practice we can only get better.'

She laughed with him, there in the quiet of the room, with a single candle flickering and the sound of the wind against glass. And for the first time in all of his life Simeon thought, *this is where I belong, right here, in this place, with this woman and at this moment.*

When he tensed at the shock of it she felt the quiver.

'Are you happy?'

'Finally I am,' he said and meant it.

She woke to find him asleep beside her, the half-dusk of the early hours around them. The candle had burnt out and a small moon was visible through a crack in the curtains.

She had gone to sleep as half a person and woken up as a whole one. That thought made tears well in her eyes and she kept absolutely still lest Simeon hear her and wonder.

He was asleep on his side and turned towards her, his eyelashes absurdly long and a half-smile on his lips. Not dangerous and menacing tonight, but almost young. She wished she might reach over and touch him so that he would wake and be there again. Speaking. Loving. Being.

A wash of wanting him came unexpectedly across her body, heating stillness, the resonance of memory bold.

And then he was awake, his eyes catching the light, her small movements bringing him from slumber.

'You sleep lightly,' she murmured.

'Mostly, I barely sleep at all,' he returned, his hand finding hers as his glance went to the window, calculating the time by the moon. 'It'll nearly be three.' He tipped his head to listen to the noises.

'I heard a church bell before?'

'St James's in Piccadilly. You will have

heard the two "new" quarter chimers, though they have been there for a while.'

'At Athelridge there are no ringing bells.'

'Just silence? I'd probably like that better.'

He rolled towards her and turned her so that the length of his body warmed her back and she felt his hardness.

'You are cold, Adelia.'

'I was just thinking the opposite.'

His hand fell down to the wetness between her legs, and she moved to allow him access.

'I don't want to hurt you.' Quiet words given in that particular clipped accent he used when he was being careful.

'You won't.'

One finger followed the next and she stretched out, wanting more, breath hitching in her throat. When he found the hard nub inside she groaned, his movements there making her understand just how easily he might rouse her.

He had the covers off them in a moment and was lifting her, so that his mouth now lay where his fingers had. The shock of what he did had her trying to stop him, but he held her hands bound behind her and carried on, the rhythm quickening and lust ruling.

She was wanton and shameless and unrestrained, the same feeling as last night rising within her until she could control nothing, but merely let herself be carried away with him to a place of only response. There were no words here or thoughts, only reaction and heat, and then tears as she fell to earth again entwined in his arms, his hand in her hair soothing, making her know that everything was just as it should be and that he would always keep her safe.

When she awoke next the sun was well up in the sky and Simeon was no longer in her bed.

She sat up in pure alarm. My God, what time was it and how had she slumbered all of these hours uninterrupted? Her next thought was of Charlotte and Flora. Had they been asking for her, had the servants seen her here in this tangle of sheets and naked, her hair a wild riot of curls all around her?

She looked down at the red marks on her breasts where he had suckled hard and at the blood that stained the bed beneath her. Not much of it, but there.

Had Simeon seen this? Would he know?

The next thought was of the night. They had

made love again after he had taken her with his mouth and again at some time in the light of dawn, slowly and languidly, without words.

She was immodest and abandoned and licentious, like her father probably, his blood running in hers and ruling flesh. Was that why Simeon had left her, a husband who had wanted a proper wife and received a bawdy lust-filled desperate bride instead?

There had been nothing mentioned of love.

Pulling her fingers through her hair, Adelia tried to tame the curls. Her lips felt swollen and dry and the place he had touched the most was sore and aching.

Wanting less? Wanting more? She could not tell. All she did know was that if he were to return right now she would open her legs and welcome him in, welcome his thickness and his heat and his clever fingers stroking places that made her rise with the promise.

She lay back in the feather pillows and pulled a silken sheet across her, enjoying the feel of the fabric on her body, sensitive from all his ministrations. With care her own fingers went where his had lingered and she writhed at the touch, wet and hot and ready.

'Simeon.' She whispered his name and felt

her nipples tighten and then the door opened and he was there, seeing all that she felt.

He shut the door quietly and locked it before turning, his fingers quickly undoing his necktie and unbuttoning his waistcoat and shirt. His shoes were off before he had gone another footfall and then his trousers. His beauty in the light of day took away her breath and she pushed back the sheets, the rise of his manhood growing before her very eyes.

So easy to want him, so effortless to simply open her legs and feel him slip in, swollen and large. When he tilted her hips she helped him edge in farther, their flesh joined completely.

He threw back his head and pumped hard and fast, no finesse this time in the face of need, no tarrying, and when he climaxed she felt the heat of it inside her. Closing her eyes, she joined him in a place that was only theirs, everything pulsating through her body, no control in it.

She was insatiable and so was he. He had noted the blood of her innocence on the sheet and seen the marks he had placed upon the pale ivory of her skin from the night before. Yet she did not rebuff him, did not close off and tell him that it was too much, this lust, and that there would be no more.

No. She had welcomed him in with her hooded eyes and her ready body, with her tight nipples and her wetness, welcomed him in and used him as he had her, with no thought to propriety or decorum or modesty.

This marriage of inconvenience had become one of a startling opportuneness that he could barely contemplate. She was a Venus wrapped in the wants of a siren. She was a modern Helen of Troy with a face that might launch a thousand nights of lust and he could not believe his luck and good fortune.

She was asleep again, he saw, her eyelashes motionless on her flushed cheeks, her hair all around them in pale and unkempt curls. She had let her guard down and the careful prickly wife who had forced him to marry her had softened and opened.

Adelia trusted him. That realisation made him smile, for he remembered arriving at his uncle's house and sleeping for a week when he first had been rescued. A sanctuary of safety, a place of hope. Was it the same for her here with him?

The gold cross she always wore caught the

light as he moved away from the bed, towards the window. She still wore his ring, too, and he smiled.

His wife. To have and to hold. For ever.

Did she love him? Could he ask?

He shook his head and placed a finger against the cold of the glass.

Could he say it to Adelia or would it frighten her? She'd wanted distance and had been most insistent on the concept of a marriage that was not in any shape or form a normal one.

Had that changed now?

Had he rushed her? Would it have been better to get to know her properly, to feel the slow rise of emotion that a girl of her standing would have been far more apt to expect?

He had taken her to his bed and deflowered her, then continued to use her time after time and hour after hour, leaving no moment for confessed closeness or love. They had barely talked at all, each joining a separate and heady copulation that had left no time for the truth.

He looked back and frowned. The bed was untidy, her nightgown strewn across the floor and the thin see-through shift she had worn was ripped along the side seams.

He remembered tugging it off her, wanting

so desperately that he had pulled too hard, the tearing egging him on and blinding him to the proper manner of taking a virgin.

Like a beast. Like a man from the world he had been born into, a rougher, turbulent and coarser world. Women like his mother had been playthings for men, females to ride on and mate with, a warm body on a cold night in a flea-filled bed, no emotion attached to the act apart from lust.

Had she thought him the same? This morning when he had come to tell her breakfast was waiting, all thoughts of food had left on the first sight of her and he had feasted on Adelia instead. The marks of desire, the blood, the quick, hard ride to orgasm, no care in any of it save completion.

Hell, he wanted her again right now even thinking of it, wanted to rouse her and enter her and know the deep damp of her inside, his seed spilling into her womb.

He'd always been so circumspect in love-making, always kept a great deal of himself back and maintained a certain distance. With Adelia he had simply vanished into her so that he could no longer tell where one of them began and the other one ended. And it came from her generosity of allowing him anything.

His hand pushed hard against a new and growing arousal.

He did not want to leave the bedroom or her bed. He should go, grab his clothes and walk out, but nothing could make him do it. Instead, he climbed under the sheet and took her into his arms, rousing her, his manhood fitting like a glove into the place between her legs.

Home. Here.

He began to move again as she did and the world about them simply fell away.

Chapter Eleven

Charlotte and Flora were full of their outing with the governess into the streets of London to purchase gifts for Simeon's birthday, which was a week away.

Adelia had not known his birthday was so close and the gaiety and humour which the girls brought back to the town house was in direct contrast to her own less certain thoughts.

She hadn't seen her husband since the morning. He had not returned for lunch when she had risen and bathed, nor for the early dinner, which the girls had partaken in. Mrs Hayward had mentioned something of a business meeting, but when he still had not returned by eight o'clock she wondered if he ever would.

She'd sat in her sitting room fully dressed with the door open and waited for him, but by eleven o'clock she could no longer stay awake, so had given up and gone to bed.

At breakfast the next morning he still had not returned and she was becoming increasingly worried.

Charlotte was telling her something of walking across to the park to pick some flowers with Flora and in the haze of concern she had nodded and watched the two girls go accompanied by the governess.

She sat there after they left and tried to pull herself together, but all she could think of was that the beautiful red-haired mistress had managed to snare her husband again and drag him back to her bed.

A foolish thought, but one that arrived and stuck. Twenty minutes later she heard a shout from the road and stood to walk to the window. The governess was suddenly there, crossing the road alone, and alarm flared. Was it safe here in this part of London or did the verdant green of the trees and the peacefulness of the area disguise something she should have known was not quite right?

Calling for Mrs Hayward, she began to walk to the front door.

'I can't see the girls, Mrs Hayward. Did they return to the house?'

'I don't think so, Mrs Morgan, but I will check.' She called to Harris, the butler, and he shook his head.

Mrs Hayward was catching Adelia's own concern just as the governess came through the door breathless and upset.

'The girls are no longer with me. I can't find them.'

Adelia was running now, picking up her skirts and making her way to the park. It was a big space, but the children knew the part of it that they were allowed to play in. In a few seconds she determined that no one was where they should be. She frantically looked further afield—St James's Park Lake was an added worry—but there wasn't a sign of anyone.

It was a punishment, she thought next, for in her life any happy moment had always been counterbalanced by an unhappy one. This was happening because of her time spent with Simeon yesterday. From the pinnacle of joy to the crashing fear of loss, no middle ground in it, only dread.

Harris was calling and so was Mrs Hayward

and the governess, their voices attracting notice until a small crowd had gathered.

No one had seen the girls. No one had noticed them leave. No one could remember any other person in the vicinity during the past hour. It was a mystery.

The sun still shone through billowing clouds, but the world had changed. She had lost them and now they were unprotected. It was her fault, her penance—there was no other way to look at it.

Simeon chose that moment to reappear and instead of rushing to his side and imploring his help she could only shout at him like some demented crone.

'Flora and Charlotte have disappeared entirely and it's our fault. This happened because of us. They have gone. For ever.'

When he came forward, she lifted her hands to ward him away.

'No. Don't touch me or we will never get them back.'

She knew it was a crazy thought, but she believed it implicitly.

'We will find them, Adelia.'

His voice was calm as he spoke with Mrs Hayward and the governess to try to put the facts of what had happened into some order, a man of control and discipline and self-restraint who had little time for histrionics.

She saw him call for the carriage and leave without looking back, even as he instructed his servants to take her back inside and watch over her.

'Charlotte,' she screamed once and then twice more, not caring who saw her or what they thought. She wanted her little sister back in her arms with a dreadful and urgent ache and she needed Flora there, too, with her dark eyes and her terrible history. A child who had been ruined by her own father's hatred.

Nothing made sense. Nothing felt real. In a few hours the dark would come and the children would be lost for ever.

Tossing off the hands of the housekeeper, she began to run towards the other side of the park. She would find them herself. She would hunt in the streets of London until she was ancient and wizened and she would not stop until she found them. There was no sense left in her, only the panic of loss. Simeon. Charlotte. Flora. All gone because of her.

* * *

Simeon returned home an hour later. Mrs Hayward met him at the door.

'Was there any sign, sir?'

'No. They were not on the other side of the park or anywhere on the main road. I went as far as Hyde Park.'

'You waded in the water, sir.' Her eyes looked at the wetness of his trousers.

'The Serpentine. I thought…' But he stopped because he did not wish to voice exactly what he thought. 'Where is my wife?'

'Your wife, sir?'

Exasperation rose. 'Mrs Morgan. Can you ask her to come down to see me please, Mrs Hayward?'

'She is not here, sir. She left directly after you did. I imagined you to be together, looking.' She stopped and took in a breath.

'You are saying she is not in the house?' he said urgently.

'I am, sir.'

'Damn it.'

He'd spent yesterday with Tom, moving him into rooms he owned in Kensington and ones more suited to his needs given the severity of his injuries. Then he had visited his old friend from Manchester and his son in White-chapel to thank them for their help in finding those responsible for Tom's injuries. One drink had led to another until at midnight he had thought it better if he stayed with them and made his way home in the morning, for he was worse for wear from drink and exhaustion.

There was another reason, of course, for such an out-of-character decision, but he did not want to dwell on his need to be away from Adelia.

He had thought that twenty-four hours would give her time to understand what had happened between them and determine which way she now wanted to proceed.

And instead he had arrived home to chaos.

'Which direction was she headed when you last saw her?'

Mrs Hayward pointed towards the park, but even as she did so a small figure could be seen walking towards them.

'Flora.'

He was out of the door and along the road without pause and the girl came into his arms crying, her eyes swollen and the skirt of her dress torn.

He lifted her up to check her, to see that there was not a worse harm, but everything seemed to be in order and he thanked the Lord for that.

'Charlotte was taken, Uncle Simeon, in the trees of the park, for he was waiting there. The man got her and dragged her away and I tried to stop him, but he was too strong, so I followed him across the main street and on to the road where the big church is with the bells. But then I did not see them again and I got lost and I could not remember where I was and everything looked different and the clouds got darker and I couldn't ask anyone how to get home because Mama said I was never to talk to strangers.'

She burst into tears and the redness of her eyes was made redder again.

'It's all right, Flora. It's all right. I know where you went and I will go and get Charlotte. It is quite all right.'

Mrs Hayward was beside them now and he carefully gave the child to her. 'Take her home and comfort her and if my wife returns make sure she stays there. Don't let her come out again. I want to know where she is and not have to worry. I will find Charlotte.'

'Very good, sir.' The child went to the housekeeper and snuggled in. For that at least Simeon was grateful.

Adelia heard the bells of Westminster Abbey chiming close by and knew a moment of panic. She had been out here for an hour searching and had found nothing, the words of a prayer recited again and again to a forgiving and loving God. *Please let me find them. Please let me find them.*

The rain was here now, small spots which she knew would become harder ones given the colour of the clouds above. Charlotte would be terrified and Adelia had always been there for her in the scary times of her life. Now she was not. Now her sister was lost in the streets of London, Flora with her, the streets where miscreants and criminals lingered and where poverty made people do things that were unspeakable.

She couldn't go back to the house empty-handed. She would never be able to go back if she could not find the girls. Desperation made her shake.

She knew who the man was the moment he approached her.

'Alexander?'

He was walking north and she knew he had come to meet her. She also knew without a doubt that he had taken the children.

'Where are they? Where are Charlotte and Flora?'

'Your sister is in my room. She wants you. She is safe. I don't know about the other girl. I didn't see her.'

The calm which she had completely and shockingly lost hold of in the park with Simeon was returning and she knew she had to remain friendly because otherwise Alexander might simply run off and she would never see Charlotte again.

Was he crazy? Had his mind tipped from his more usual oddness into something else entirely? Could he have hurt Charlotte? *Please God, please make her be unhurt.* Her fingers reached for the gold cross, a prayer on her lips.

'Take me to her, Alexander. I need to see her.'

She followed him, because to do anything else might relegate her sister to being gone for ever. But as he went he stopped to speak with a man who was selling food near the Abbey. A girl hawking flowers sat on the road nearby and, wrenching off her cross and chain, Adelia pressed the piece into surprised hands.

'Go to Carlton House Terrace to the house on the corner and ask for Mr Morgan. Give him this and he will pay you well, I swear he will. More than you will make by pawning it. Much more. Please. Tell him where you saw me.'

Alex had turned now and Adelia walked on, not looking back just in case he realised she had sought help. Her hands were shaking and she wrapped her arms around herself and swallowed, summoning calm, praying for deliverance.

The room they finally arrived at was tiny and dank, a small table in the middle and an unmade bed to one side.

Charlotte was tied to the bedpost with a long leather strap, her face white with fear as Adelia reached for her, a gag of blue fabric stuffed into her mouth.

'I am here to take you home, Charlotte.' Adelia's fingers pulled at the leather and then at the fabric, one nail tearing in her haste. She couldn't believe that Alexander hadn't stopped her from freeing her sister and only when she had done so did she turn to face him.

'We were always meant to be together, Adelia, you know that now, don't you? Your mother told me as much and the money you sent to me was confirmation.' His voice was high and desperate.

Adelia did her very best to smile.

'Of course I do.'

'But you went and did not come back.'

'I can come back now, Alexander, since you are here, and we will go home. Charlotte must be sent away, though, for Mr Morgan will stop at nothing to find her. He does not care for me, but my sister is a different story altogether. Is there someone here who could be trusted to accompany her home to Carlton House Terrace and see her safe?'

Alexander put his head out of the door and called, and a stout, kind-faced woman appeared.

'Mrs White, I need your help.' He fumbled in a purse at his waist for coin and handed her a generous amount. 'Will you take this girl back to Carlton House Terrace, for I am leaving London immediately. Do you know this street?'

'I do, sir.'

Her eyes flickered across to where Adelia

stood. She managed a smile to allay any alarm and the woman relaxed. All Adelia wanted was for Charlotte to be taken to safety and away from Alexander. She would deal with her own security after her sister had left. She was crying now more loudly and Adelia held her close before letting go, but while Alexander was distracted she whispered to her sister.

'You need to listen, Charlotte. You need to do this for me. Tell Mr Morgan where I am. Tell him to come and find me. And tell him to hurry.' She pulled the emerald ring from her finger and closed it inside her sister's fingers for safekeeping. She did not want Alex to see it as a symbol of Simeon's claim on her and become enraged.

Charlotte nodded, the pale curls the exact colour of her own coming loose from the tie that held them.

Then she was gone, and Alex loomed before her again, watchful and strange.

If she could keep him talking, the flower girl might deliver her cross to Simeon and he would come looking for her. With any luck he would find Charlotte on the way back. At least the children would be safe.

The clouds had begun to thicken and it felt

colder. Without a cloak or shawl she shivered, and Alex reached for the blanket on the bed and wrapped it around her.

'We will find transport when we can, but we will leave now. It is dangerous here for us. Hold my hand, my love, and I will help you.'

She gave him her fingers, but was not prepared for what happened next. He had retrieved the tie on the bed and he now wrapped the leather around her arm and tethered it to his.

'For safety,' he said as she looked up at him. But she could see other darker things there crawling in his eyes and she knew that going anywhere with him was a dangerous thing to do.

He caught her chin with his fist even as she struggled and then all she knew was blackness.

'There is a street seller at the door, sir.'

Harris's voice broke into Simeon's quest to find a warmer cloak and sturdier boots before going out again. 'She has Mrs Morgan's gold cross in her hands and asks to see you.'

He was at the door in a moment, the girl who stood there young and scared.

'The pretty lady said to give it to a Mr Morgan and that he would pay me.'

'Where and when did she give it to you?'

'At the front of the Abbey, sir, about an hour ago. She said I was to come straight here and so I did, but it took me a while to see to it that my flowers were left somewhere safe and then I had to find the house.'

'Who was she with?'

'A man, sir. A tall man with brown hair and blue eyes and he spoke nice. She were following him, sir. They were going south when last I saw them.'

'Did she look scared?'

'A bit, I think, though she were trying not to show it. She weren't altogether happy, though. The man stopped at the barrow by the main path and he got some food. He were in a hurry 'cos he told old Vern to quicken it up. He had a bite on his hand and there were blood, though he'd tried to hide it with the cuff of his jacket, but I notice those things.'

'Was there anything else?'

'No, sir. I didn't see nothing else at all.'

Simeon handed over two gold coins and the mouth of the small flower seller dropped open, her hands snatching the bounty before it was taken away and running down the stairs and up the street, ragged skirts twitching.

He had a lead and it was a good one. He knew vaguely where Adelia had been taken.

Grabbing his hat, he strode out of the door, understanding now just what fear truly was. If he lost her... No he could not think like that.

Her last words to him in the park were worrying, but then she was out of her mind with concern and blaming their intimacy and happiness on all the mayhem transpiring. Did she truly think that their joy in the marriage bed was the reason for the children's misfortune?

He could not think of this now. He needed to concentrate on finding his wife and her sister and bringing them home to safety.

Fifteen minutes later he spotted Charlotte along Birdcage Walk beside a woman and crying. When he stopped the carriage and leapt out, she began to run towards him, falling into his arms with relief just as Flora had done, tears streaming down her cheeks.

'Mr Thompson has Adelia. He made her come with him. She gave me this.' The ring was placed in his hand. 'She wants you to come and find her.'

'Where is she?'

'In a small room that this woman, Mrs White, rents out.'

He turned to the older lady looking on with amazement.

'What is the address of your house?'

'On Great Peter Street, sir. Near the corner of Horseferry Road. The man came two days ago and has hardly been home until today when he brought back the girl. I didn't know nothing of any of it, sir. He paid me for the lodging and said he was leaving London. They won't be there any more, I don't think.' She gave him the number of the house, though, just in case.

'Can you take Charlotte back to Carlton House Terrace and deliver her safely home, Mrs White?'

'I can, sir.'

Another few gold coins were dispatched and then he left them. The weather was worsening and he had only a few hours left until dusk.

He found the house the woman had mentioned, but on looking through the rooms he saw no sign of anybody. A youth near the front door said he'd seen the couple leave, the man carrying the woman because she was sick. He gave their direction as a southern one.

Fear congealed in Simeon's throat. If the bastard had hurt Adelia, he would kill him. His fingers clutched the hilt of the knife he had taken from the drawer in his library and he felt the man he used to be return suddenly and completely. Cold. Hard. Violent.

Sending the carriage back, he scoured the smaller alleys about him for signs of his wife, but ever moving southwards. The rain was falling now, but he barely noticed it. She would be here somewhere, he knew it, because anyone on the run would use the daylight hours to travel. Perhaps Thompson was making for someone he knew or perhaps he just felt this direction was a better one to put people off his trail. Simeon had expected him to strike out north.

His first luck came when a beggar sitting in a doorway gestured to him.

'If you be looking for the man who is dragging a woman behind him and has blood on his shirt, he went that way, sir, about half an hour ago. I knew someone would be along to look for them soon and you have the face of one who is.'

'Was she walking?'

'Dragging her feet a bit. There was a

strap holding them together, which I thought strange...'

He tossed the man a coin and hurried on.

An hour later he found them, tucked in under a shelter and around a fire with a number of other men, men without their own abodes, rough-looking and unfriendly.

Adelia was wrapped in a blanket and was just sitting there, the tie the beggar had mentioned dangling from her left arm. The one whom he presumed was Alexander Thompson spoke to the others, though Simeon noticed he often looked over his shoulder at her. He was a tall man and surprisingly big.

Understanding the lie of the land, Simeon moved forward, his cloak billowing in the rising breeze.

'I am here to take my wife home,' he said firmly when he was close enough and all the faces turned, reminding him so forcibly of his childhood scraps that he almost smiled.

Adelia stood, her face disbelieving, but Thompson stopped her.

'She's with me now.'

'No.' She tried to run towards him, but Thompson caught at the long leather tie and pulled her back off her feet. She fell hard on the cobbled road as Simeon charged, catching the man unawares and pinning him against a wall behind before slamming him in the face.

Another fellow was there now, his fists raised, and lifting his leg Simeon kicked back hard, the second offender going down in a heap behind him and staying there. The third man was easier again. A slam across the face and a push and he was out. With his attention off Thompson for a few seconds, though, the man had grabbed a piece of wood beside him, the weight of it brought down across Simeon's back with a crunch.

Adelia screamed, but even pain meant little as he delivered a right upper cut to Thompson's chin.

This time he knew the man was finished with and he simply left him there, unconscious on the road with the rain on his face, and strode across to his wife.

They came together hard, his hands on her, tracing the bruise on her chin gently.

'He hit you?'

His old accent was back, but he could not seem to find the new one. 'Did he hurt you anywhere else?'

She shook her head and simply clung to him. The other men about the fire had scurried away and all that was left now around them were the inert bodies of the three men who had challenged them.

Then a constable was there and others milling about to see what had happened. When Simeon told the man his story he went straight over to Alexander Thompson, who was just coming to with a groan, and lifted him to his feet. Another constable had joined him, too, and the pair of them heaved him off, but not before asking for Simeon's name and address.

'Can you walk to the main road?' He asked Adelia this quietly. 'I can find a cab there to take us home.'

Five minutes later he waved down a hackney and they slipped inside, the silence welcomed, all threat gone.

Giving the driver his address, he drew in a breath before turning to Adelia.

She held on to him, her fingers clutching at his clothes as if they might never let go.

'Is Charlotte…?'

'Home and safe. A woman brought her back.'

Adelia hated her tears, but try as she might

she could not stop them from coming. It was the shock, she thought, and the sudden relief to be here, safe, with Simeon.

'Why did Thompson do it?' She knew this question would come from him, but she had no true answer.

'All that he said was that he got too lonely and had come to London to find me. He said he loved me and that I loved him. He said it over and over again, for he is mad, I think, and blames everyone around him for his problems.' Her voice broke, and she swallowed, trying to get the next words out. 'I hoped beyond hope that you'd find me, but I couldn't believe it when you came, Simeon. I looked up and there you were in the shadow of the fire and rain and you fought them all so easily.'

'It's one of the things Angel Meadow teaches you. If you don't learn that, then you don't live long.'

Her hands were on his face, checking for damage, and then his lips came down on hers, warm and safe in a world that was not. They were both alive and together and that was all that mattered. Just them.

It was a careful kiss, a gentle kiss, the violence of the past hours far from this tenderness. He kissed her as if she was breakable and fragile and in a sense she was.

'I have always been afraid,' she said when he pulled back, her head fitting in the space beneath his chin and in the place above his heart. She liked listening to the beat for it pulled her back into life. 'Ever since I can remember my fear has got in the way of everything. It did again...today...in the park. I thought it was my fault, that the happiness you gave to me was why Charlotte and Flora had been lost. But you can't hold your breath for that long or keep on thinking that it is your fault without dying inside and I think I did that, too, died inside, until yesterday, until the night before last.'

Now that she had started to speak she could not stop, for she wanted him to understand her more than anything.

'I have to live again and not be afraid. I have to know that I am worth it, Simeon, that I am a person who is worth it and that I am enough.'

She wondered if she was making sense or if he thought her as mad as Alexander? She was glad that it was dark and that they were alone and that they were not yet back at the town house with all of the questions she knew would be waiting there. 'You are not afraid of anything and I admire that.'

He laughed quietly, she could hear the rumble of it in his chest. 'Everyone has things that scare them, Adelia. If you didn't, you wouldn't be human.'

'What are you frightened of most, then?'

'Losing you.'

Two words she could not believe he had said. 'Me?'

He placed her aside and knelt on the carriage floor, finding her ring in his pocket and holding it in his fingers so that she could see it.

'Would you marry me, Adelia Hermione Josephine Bennett?'

'I already have. Once.'

He smiled and tried again. 'Give me your hand.'

His fingers were cold as he placed the ring on the fourth finger and pushed it down.

'Last time it was a forced choice. This time it's because I love you, Adelia.'

'You love me?'

'With all my heart and soul.'

Her tears were becoming a nuisance, but as she folded her hand around his ring she knew a permanence that was true and honest.

'I love you, Simeon, and I will for ever.'

And then he rose and kissed her again, holding her on his knee, his lips brushing away both hurt and fear.

'So I'll take that as a yes?'

'Yes. Yes. Yes.'

He loved her and she loved him back and it was not a small love, but a huge, big, all-encompassing one of shared opinion and respect. And lust, she added with an inward smile, as she felt him beneath her, his body saying things that were easy to interpret.

'When did you know you first loved me, Simeon?'

'At the dinner party when you held me in your arms and taught me to waltz.'

Delight assailed her.

'What of you? When did you know?'

'I think I always knew. From our first meeting when you held me close. I dreamed every night of you again and again and when you said nothing of my foolishness in coming to your town house alone despite my lies and deceit...' She hesitated before continuing. 'We have wasted so much time...'

He began to laugh. 'But no longer. From

now on we will enjoy every moment of being together.'

He kissed her then softly, careful of her bruised chin. He kissed her as though she was made of china and infinitely precious.

'I have your cross at home, Adelia.' He said this after a few moments. 'A young flower seller brought it back.'

'All these people who have helped us.'

'See, the world is not as bad as you think it. With love there is always a way home.'

'Take me there now, Simeon. I want to hold the girls and afterwards...' She stopped, her heart beginning to thump more quickly.

'We will go to bed and celebrate our marriage properly?'

'You promise?'

'With all my heart.'

Epilogue

Richmond, 1843

It was Christmas Eve and the snow in Richmond was thick on the ground, the river steel grey and the trees brown and bare.

The fire in the main sitting room overlooking the vista blazed under a mantel of wide hewn stone. A solid and simple house, just as Simeon had promised.

Charlotte and Flora were in their beds full of excitement for tomorrow, and Jamie lay in his cot nearby, asleep at last. At six months old their small son was the spitting image of his father, though his eyes were hers, clear emerald green and startling in the brown hue of his skin. The girls adored him and even her mother who came down often to visit from Athelridge Hall was beginning to look happier.

The ghosts of the past had been pushed away and were being replaced by living and breathing family and the promise of a future which looked bright.

Adelia sat in Simeon's lap in her nightgown, watching the flame, his arms holding her close, one hand cupping her stomach.

They were expecting their second child in six months, the surprise of him or her still delighting them.

'We will have a whole brood of children here one day at this rate, my love. A small tribe of Morgans who will keep us busy.' Simeon said this in a teasing tone, but she could hear pride in every word.

'Well, the house is certainly big enough,' she returned and brought his fingers up to kiss them one by one. 'And we have more than enough love to share around.'

'Tom Brady is coming up in the morning, did I tell you that? He is off to America in February and he tells me he wants to find a wife as suitable as my own.'

'Suitable?' She frowned.

'Functional. Fertile. Convenient.'

She laughed at all the words he gave her. 'None of those descriptions sound very flattering.'

'Then how about beautiful, clever, sensual and brave?'

'Oh, I like those much better.'

His hand moved down and he lifted up her hem. He knew that she wore only her skin under her nightgown.

'It's quiet and late and the baby is asleep.' There was joy in his words.

'And the servants have all gone to their families 'til the morrow.' She added this as he turned her around, feeling his hardness like an ache as he slipped inside her.

Paradise. A home, a family and a husband who had stopped her being afraid and made her feel safe and wanted instead.

She smiled as he quickened his movements and the flame built. Her breasts were full and her nipples were darker and the marks left on her skin from Jamie's birth were visible in the firelight. Yet she had never felt more beautiful, more whole, more complete in her life.

'Love me, Simeon.'

'It's for ever.' He whispered this and then there were no more words between them as their flesh heated and they took each other to heaven.

* * * * *

COMING SOON!

We really hope you enjoyed reading this book.
If you're looking for more romance, be sure to
head to the shops when new books are
available on

Thursday 28th
May

MILLS & BOON

Coming next month

FROM CINDERELLA TO COUNTESS
Annie Burrows

All of a sudden, a solution came to him.

A solution so dazzlingly brilliant he didn't know why it hadn't occurred to him before. He'd always known he *ought* to marry, for the sake of the succession. The prospect had hung over him like a black cloud ever since he'd learned that his primary function in life was to sire the next generation. But the prospect of marrying a "suitable" girl, for dynastic reasons, had always seemed cold and cheerless. The alternative, marrying for love, had been equally repellent. And so he'd declared, loudly and often, that he would never marry.

But what if marriage was not based on either of those two alternatives? What if he could find a middle way? What if he married a girl he liked? A girl like Miss Mitcham? A sensible, decent girl who would see all the advantages of marrying for practical reasons. A girl who wouldn't make outrageous demands upon him.

And then another aspect of things sprang to mind.

"Why not make Lady Bradbury's worst fears come to pass?" That would teach her to think she could interfere in his private life.

"In, er, what way?"

"Don't be stupid." She wasn't usually this slow on the uptake. She must know what he meant. "By marrying me, of course."

"What?" Eleanor's heart squeezed at hearing her first proposal of marriage coupled with an insult to her intelligence. Besides, from the wicked gleam in his eye, it looked as though he was joking. "That isn't funny."

"It isn't? Oh, I think it is an excellent jest, as well as being one in the eye for Lady Bradbury," he said, stepping closer and taking hold of her upper arms. Not tightly, the way he'd done before, but gently. Almost as though he was handling fragile porcelain which he didn't want to damage. "Wouldn't you like to take some revenge upon my great-aunt," he said, caressingly. Running his thumbs up and down her arms in an equally caressing manner.

"I don't think revenge is a good reason for getting married," she said. Although her heart was pounding as fast as if she'd been running. Because he was tugging her closer to his body. Until she could feel the heat blazing from him.

Continue reading
FROM CINDERELLA TO COUNTESS
Annie Burrows

Available next month
www.millsandboon.co.uk

LET'S TALK
Romance

For exclusive extracts, competitions
and special offers, find us online:

f facebook.com/millsandboon

🐦 @MillsandBoon

📷 @MillsandBoonUK

Get in touch on 01413 063232

For all the latest titles coming soon, visit
millsandboon.co.uk/nextmonth

MILLS & BOON

THE HEART OF ROMANCE

A ROMANCE FOR EVERY KIND OF READER

MODERN

Prepare to be swept off your feet by sophisticated, sexy and seductive heroes, in some of the world's most glamourous and romantic locations, where power and passion collide.
8 stories per month.

HISTORICAL

Escape with historical heroes from time gone by. Whether your passion is for wicked Regency Rakes, muscled Vikings or rugged Highlanders, awaken the romance of the past.
6 stories per month.

MEDICAL

Set your pulse racing with dedicated, delectable doctors in the high-pressure world of medicine, where emotions run high and passion, comfort and love are the best medicine.
6 stories per month.

True Love

Celebrate true love with tender stories of heartfelt romance, from the rush of falling in love to the joy a new baby can bring, and a focus on the emotional heart of a relationship.
8 stories per month.

Desire

Indulge in secrets and scandal, intense drama and plenty of sizzling hot action with powerful and passionate heroes who have it all: wealth, status, good looks…everything but the right woman.
6 stories per month.

HEROES

Experience all the excitement of a gripping thriller, with an intense romance at its heart. Resourceful, true-to-life women and strong, fearless men face danger and desire - a killer combination!
8 stories per month.

DARE

Sensual love stories featuring smart, sassy heroines you'd want as a best friend, and compelling intense heroes who are worthy of them
4 stories per month.

To see which titles are coming soon, please visit
millsandboon.co.uk/nextmonth